A
HEAVENLY
DEATH

A HEAVENLY DEATH

The Frank May Chronicles

Lawrence Friedman

A QP Mystery

QP BOOKS
New Orleans, Louisiana

A HEAVENLY DEATH
The Frank May Chronicles

A QP Mystery, published in 2014 by QP Books.

QUID PRO, LLC
5860 Citrus Blvd., Suite D-101
New Orleans, Louisiana 70123
www.qpbooks.com

ISBN 978-1-61027-276-6 (paperback)
ISBN 978-1-61027-277-3 (eBook)

Publisher's Cataloging-in-Publication

Friedman, Lawrence.
    A Heavenly Death / Lawrence Friedman.
        p. cm.
    Series: *The Frank May Chronicles* (#8)
    ISBN 978-1-61027-276-6 (pbk)
1. Lawyers—California—Fiction. 2. San Mateo (Cal.)—Fiction. 3. May, Frank (Fictitious character)—Fiction. I. Friedman, Lawrence. II. Title. III. Series.
PS357.F788 2014   813.'1'8552—dc22
                                              20145411837
                                                  CIP

for Leah, Jane, Amy, Sarah,
David, Lucy, and Irene

A

HEAVENLY

DEATH

1

When you practice law, which is what I do for a living, you expect to meet all kinds of people ... and of course you do. Some of these people are lovable, some of them are annoying; some are ordinary, and some are pretty strange. I would have put Morris Gross into the ordinary category—at least at first. Morris was a short, pudgy man; he had fat fingers, and was slightly bow-legged. He was quite bald, except for some fringes on the sides, which he obviously combed to make his head less egg-like. He was in his early 60's. He was a bachelor, and to the best of my knowledge, had always been a bachelor. He had a monotonous voice, although at times it seemed to squeak. He was stingy, and seemed suspicious of everybody and everything. Moreover, he seemed, quite frankly, rather boring.

But there were three things about Morris that were hardly boring. The first was his money. Morris had a great deal of money—money he inherited from his mother. He also inherited the luxurious condo in Palo Alto where he had lived, together with his aged mother, for many years. When she died, at 94, she left all her money to her son, Morris.

If you have enough money, you're automatically interesting. And the more money you have the more interesting you become. I imagine that nobody with a billion dollars is truly uninteresting. You also can't be boring if you hold a certain position in life. The Queen of Denmark, for example, cannot possibly be boring, no matter what she's like in private life. The Queen of England, I have to admit, is *almost* boring—but then, as I said, no queen (or king) can be boring. Morris, of course,

1

was neither a king nor a queen, nor President of the United States, or anything else that would have made him per se non-boring. Nor was he a billionaire. But he was very rich, and that lent him a certain aura, like the halo around the head of a saint. Of course, Morris Gross was not a saint.

He did have a second feature that definitely took him out of the boring category. It was the story he told me, sitting in my office in San Mateo, California, in a chair right across from my desk. It was such an astonishing story that it made me wonder whether Morris had become, well, somewhat demented. I had never yet heard such a story, in all my years of practicing law. It was definitely a first. I'll tell you about this story in a bit. I do want to mention the third thing, though, which made Morris exceptionally non-boring. It was this: one evening, quite unexpectedly, when Morris Gross was at home in his condo, someone shot him dead, and left him lying on the floor. The police called it murder.

My first reaction to this startling news was to wonder: could Morris's death be possibly connected to the strange tale he told me in my office? But I mustn't get ahead of my story.

I have to introduce myself. My name is Frank May; I'm 45 years old, married, two children (girls, both in high schools). My wife's name is Celia. She teaches in a local high school. I'm a member of the California bar. I'm in the general practice of law, but a great deal of my practice has to do with wills, trusts, estate planning—that sort of thing. I also represent a number of small businesses: an Armenian restaurant owner, for example. I mean, the man who runs the place is Armenian; the restaurant doesn't serve Armenian food, whatever that might be. It's mostly hamburgers and the like. Anyway, he has nothing to do with this story.

I'm a solo practitioner, which means simply that I have no partners. My office is located in San Mateo, California—and San Mateo, for those not lucky enough to live in California, is a suburb of San Francisco, some miles south of the city itself, on the San Francisco Peninsula. People love San Francisco, which is a major tourist attraction. No tourist ever comes to San

Mateo. Why should they? But it's a terrific place to have an office. In any event, that's where I am.

* * *

To get back to my story: I'll never forget the day when Morris's niece, Felicity Gross, called me on the phone, and broke the news: she told me that Morris Gross was dead. I was absolutely stunned. I had drafted a new will for Morris Gross, which he had signed about a year before; more recently, I had drafted a brand-new will to replace it. He had never gotten around to signing this will—I'll tell you more about that later. And now he was dead.

"My God, Felicity. I'm so terribly sorry," I said. "I can't believe it. Was it his heart? I mean, he had this massive heart attack last year."

"No, Frank," she said. "It's something else. It's completely awful. Somebody killed him."

"Killed him? What on earth do you mean, Felicity?"

"I mean, killed him. Shot him. He was murdered, Frank."

"My God," I said again. "Who did it? Was it a burglar?"

"I don't know, Frank," she said. "They don't think so. No sign of that. And they didn't find the gun. Not that that matters, I suppose. We're all in shock."

"I can imagine," I said.

When I put down the phone, I couldn't help thinking about Morris Gross. The late Morris Gross. As I told you, I had worked on his will. He came to my office a number of times. He usually came by taxi, from his condo in Palo Alto. He always grumbled about how much he had to pay the taxi-driver. Once, his niece, Felicity, brought him. She was a handsome woman, in her 30's, I would say, with dark hair, almost shoe-polish black, which I think she dyed; tall, and rather elegantly dressed. She explained that Morris didn't like to drive. His parents had once had a car, but after Morris's father died, they sold it. Felicity said she'd come back and pick him up, when we were through with our business.

When she left, Morris sat down and started to talk about his will. He said he was in something of a hurry—clients always are—so I took notes, and when Felicity came back, and they left, I worked on the draft, and got it ready for him. Not that Morris's will presented any particular problem. I'll get back to that point later. And to be honest, we lawyers never write a will from scratch. A lot of the provisions—we call them "boiler plate"—are things we stick into every will we write. The only clauses we actually write fresh are the so-called "dispositive" clauses, the ones where we say who gets what; and usually this is pretty easy too. I've had complex, awkward wills and trusts, but Morris's wasn't one of those.

I pictured Morris, in my office, sitting across from my desk. As I think I mentioned, I never liked him particularly. Morris was the youngest son of Bertha Gross; and her favorite, for some unaccountable reason. Or perhaps it was because, unlike his two sisters and his brother, he never married, and never worked, for at least the last twenty years of Bertha's life. He lived in his mother's lavish condo which was located, as I said, in Palo Alto. The condo was on Alma Street, in a high rise; Bertha's flat was near the top of the building. It had a beautiful view, or as beautiful as a view could be when all you saw were the rooftops of Palo Alto—it was certainly not like looking at the Golden Gate Bridge, or the mountains . . . or the rooftops of Paris. Bertha's condo was a double flat; she and her late husband Henry bought two apartments on the same floor when they moved in. They broke down the wall between them, and created a single large and spacious apartment.

Of course, at that time, I had never actually seen this condo. Later, I would pay a visit—but this was after Morris was dead. It was one of the nicest buildings in Palo Alto, mostly full of elderly, rich widows. There was an exercise room in the basement, which probably got very little use, at least from the occupants, and a large lobby full of sleek, sterile, and expensive furniture, all chrome and glass. Nobody ever sat down there except a man in uniform, who more or less kept watch on who went in and out, but mostly seemed to sit at a desk quietly dozing off.

At any rate, Bertha's husband died shortly after they moved in, and Morris replaced him. Or maybe he lived there already; I never learned much about his early life. From then on, Morris shared the condo with his mother. And shared her life. Felicity described to me, later on, what that life was like. Morris and Bertha played gin rummy in the evenings, at least when Bertha was in the mood. At other times, they sat and watched television. They had two large Lazy-Boy easy chairs, side by side, in front of a giant television set. In the afternoon, Bertha indulged in her favorite soap operas; she also liked to watch Judge Judy and the other judge programs, where dim-witted people come and wash their dirty linen in public. In the evening, Bertha preferred quiz shows like "Wheel of Fortune." Morris also did chores for her, shopping at the local upscale grocery, taking her to the dentist and to the Palo Alto Clinic, whenever they had a doctor's appointment. They had no car, as I said, but they used taxis. Taxi drivers hated them because they never gave much of a tip.

Bertha was already an old lady when she became a widow and Morris either moved in, or took over a new role, I'm not sure which. Bertha of course got older and older (people do that); she also got more and more feeble with the passage of time. And more irascible. And stingier. Morris used to take her and her walker for short trips around the block. She was all skin and bones by that time, with tufts of white hair sticking up, and a grim look on her face. I heard most of this second hand, of course; from Felicity, or, later, from her brother Sebastian. Another source was one of my neighbors, who was some kind of distant cousin of the late Henry Gross. I personally never had the pleasure of meeting Bertha Gross.

Anyway, Bertha eventually became too feeble even for a walker; but even at the end, at age 94, which was when she died, confined to her home, and toward the very end, much of the time in bed, she had her wits about her. Felicity was quite frank about what her grandmother was like. She was, Felicity said, a "mean old woman, honestly, she had to have her own way. She ordered Morris about as if he was some sort of household slave. She didn't care for anybody or anything, really. And she just got meaner and feebler and more penny-pinching. I thought she was basically, as they say, too mean to die. I hate saying things like that about my grandmother. But true is true. And then she finally died."

I suppose at one time, Morris had had some sort of actual job, but I can't for the life of me imagine what it was. He had no obvious talent or ambition. Certainly, during the Bertha years, he was unemployed; not that he was looking for work. His job was Bertha. It paid off. Bertha was a very rich woman, thanks to her late husband. I have no idea what he did, but whatever it was, it made a pile of money. Bertha was a cautious investor, I guess, or else she had excellent advice. I think her estate was worth something on the order of $50,000,000. Which is real money, even in Silicon Valley, where the dream of every geek with acne and thick coke-bottle glasses, and who drops out of college, is to amass a billion dollars before age thirty, and a few of them actually accomplish this laudable goal. Morris never founded a start-up company, never did anything much at all. Morris inherited his money, and I inherited him.

Well, inherited is not quite right. Our neighbor, the distant cousin, went to Bertha's funeral, and afterwards, she had a talk with Morris. He said he needed a lawyer. She suggested me. She said my fees were reasonable, which was apparently all that Morris cared about. Of course, she had no idea whether my fees were reasonable or not; she just said so because she thought *I* was reasonable. And because she was fond of my wife, Celia; and because we had been so understanding about an issue concerning an oak tree and a huge acacia. They were our trees, but their big branches hung over her property, and she wanted to get rid of the overhanging branches, for some reason or other. We said, sure. Not only that, we paid for the work ourselves, even though I personally didn't care one way or the other about those branches. I even considered cutting down the acacia. It has beautiful flowers, but they seem to make people sneeze.

At any rate, this neighbor recommended me, and Morris made an appointment and came to see me in my office. He told me that he was "changing lawyers," as he put it. "My late mother used this one lawyer for years, Everett Mills; he did her will, and other things. I let him handle the estate. Mother had a large estate. I never liked the man. I don't like lawyers in general. Don't take that the wrong way. But this guy, well, he knew Mother's business, you know, the things she owned, and he was familiar with the estate, and I didn't want to start something new, you know what I mean, he was there already, he had the will in his office or wherever he kept it. So I just went along, I used him."

"Of course," I said.

"But I didn't like what he did. He took advantage of me," Morris said. "He had this fancy office, fancy pictures on the wall, fancy rugs on the floor—that should have given me a clue. He charged me an arm and a leg. I said to him, Everett, we're not billionaires, and that's a lot of money you're asking for. A lot of money. Like, what did you do for that money? Thousands and thousands. He said, what he charged, that was the law. I didn't believe him; what kind of a law was that? I said, well, it seems too much, I don't know why the law should tell you what to charge, and he said, oh but it does. So I said, I want an itemized bill, how many hours you spent, that sort of thing."

I nodded. There are in fact, statutory fee scales; and Everett was entitled to charge a fee based on those statutory scales. Of course, there was no law making it a crime to charge *less*, but I don't blame Everett for failing to point this out. Frankly, I would have charged the statutory fees myself—why not? It was a big estate, and the estate could afford a decent lawyer's fee. But of course I didn't tell Morris any of this.

Morris, it seemed to me, did not have what one might call a brilliant mind. He had a kind of peasant cunning, I suppose. Now he was suddenly quite rich. For all those years, he lived off Bertha's money; and I'm sure she doled it out in teaspoons. She was the type. She dominated Morris, that was clear. He had no money except whatever Bertha gave him; as long as she was competent, she paid the bills. Later on, when she was weak and sick, he asked her if she needed help, and he offered to handle her checkbook, and so on. But she refused absolutely. "But Mother, you can't handle it anymore," he said. And she said, "well, then, let Sheppard do it." Sheppard was her accountant, a man with an office in Los Gatos. Morris lived in Bertha's condo and took care of her physical needs, but she never seemed to trust him with anything that related to money. Basically, he had an allowance. Morris was not even eligible for Social Security: he had never earned enough to qualify. But that was then. Now she was dead, and Morris was seriously rich.

Rich people need wills and trusts; they need estate planning; and I was happy to fill this role for Morris Gross. I didn't have that many clients as rich as Morris. I could almost smell the fees—no, I wasn't thinking what I would make handling his estate when he was dead; he wasn't that old, after all. But estate planning, doing his will, drafting trusts—that could bring in welcome money. Don't get me wrong. I'm not greedy. I'm an honest lawyer. I know many people think that's a self-cancelling phrase, like military justice; but not all of us are parasites, bottom-feeders, blood-suckers. We do an honest job. Most of us. At any rate, I listened closely to what Morris had to say. He intended to leave the bulk of his estate to his relatives. "I've got two sisters, and six nieces and nephews. My brother Charlie's dead, poor soul, but Anna's alive, and Martha. I want those two, and Charlie's children, to have the estate. Charlie had three children: Felicity, Julia, and Sebastian."

So far, so good. That made sense. One third to each of the two sisters, and one-ninth to each of Charlie's children. "My brother Charlie," he said. "I wish he was still here. Those three kids—the two girls, Felicity and Julia, they're OK. Sebastian, well, he doesn't deserve it: lazy, good-for-nothing lout. Still, he's my nephew. Charlie would want me to take care of him."

He went on and on about his family. Not that it was the least bit relevant. But Morris felt some sort of urge to explain it all, in wearisome detail.

"Mother, well, she never really approved of my brother Charlie. He was always getting into trouble. Even in high school. College too. He cheated on an exam; and they caught him; kicked him out of college. Community college. Mother didn't want to pay for anything else, not that Charlie could get into a place like Stanford. They caught him once, trying to steal something from a hardware store. I don't remember what it was. Then he married this woman, she was a receptionist or something, worked for an investment company, answered the phone, that sort of thing; her name was Edna, and Mother said, she was trash, and frankly she was pregnant when they got married. Mother said, this woman is no good, Charlie, she's trailer trash. Well, actually, Edna never lived in any trailer. They had these three children, Felicity, Julia, and then the boy, Sebastian. Wasn't a happy marriage, Mother was right, as usual. She left him once, I think she went off with a vacuum cleaner salesman, but she came back. And then she died. Charlie, poor guy, had trouble holding a job, went from one thing to another, started a business, Mother lent him money, against her better judgment, and he lost it all. Then he married this other woman. Jasmine, She was twenty years younger than he was, Mother was very angry with him, she said, Charlie, you're a fool, you're making another colossal mistake. I won't have it. Marrying some floozy you met in a bar. Look at the clothes she wears, she looks like some sort of cheap tramp. Mother, I love her he said. She said, don't give me that love stuff. Is she pregnant? He said, Mother, how could you? No, she isn't. Then break it off, Mother said. You marry that woman, and I won't speak to you again as long as I live. But he married her anyway. Mother never spoke to him again. She had strong ideas, Mother."

"And now he's dead," I said, for want of anything better.

"Oh yes. As I said, Mother wouldn't speak to him, and of course I went along with Mother. I told him, Charlie, you're my brother, but you know what Mother said. Mother was right, naturally. That woman was no good. She was a tramp. God knows why she married Charlie. I think she thought she would get her hands on some of Mother's money. Poor Charlie, he told her his mother was filthy rich. That was a terrible mistake. Jasmine, she had no intention of being a stepmother, you know? She didn't want the kids, and they hated her. Sebastian in particular. He said he was going to make a voodoo doll, stick pins in it, and get rid of her. Told her that to her face. Of course she thought he wasn't serious. You haven't met Sebastian. He was in high school then. In a way, he was like Charlie, he looked like Charlie, and he was in trouble trouble trouble, just like

Charlie, but I think he was always smarter than Charlie. Charlie could never do his homework, you know, when we were kids. Sebastian, he was a bright boy, went to college somewhere. Anyway, back to Jasmine: I honestly believe Sebastian made that voodoo doll, and it worked, in a way. She felt death coming, I swear. She was afraid. She walked out on Charlie, just like Edna did, and that was the end of her. No idea where she is. Maybe she's dead. My sister Anna, she's an angel, she helped raise the kids, treated them just like she treated her own children, when their mother died, and even when Jasmine was in the picture."

"How nice," I said, smiling. "Those kids must have loved her."

"Who? Jasmine?"

"No. Their Aunt Anna."

But Morris shook his head. "They didn't. Kids nowadays, they have no gratitude. They take everything for granted. Anna, she knocked herself out. And they just sassed her, and resented her. Well, not Julia. But Sebastian. Really, Sebastian was awful to her. Someday they'll appreciate what she did. And their father too. Poor Charlie. Dead and gone."

What struck me was that Morris, going on and on about his family, never said anything that sounded like empathy or affection. Except for his late mother, and perhaps his sister Anna. Possibly Julia, one of his nieces. The rest, he complained about, and criticized endlessly.

Nonetheless, they were going to get his money. He wanted me to be executor, and we talked about that. I was honest about what this entailed. An executor can charge a fee; and so can the lawyer for the estate. Morris made it clear I couldn't have both fees; and I said that was perfectly alright. I suggested he might want a family member to serve as co-executor—especially since he didn't know me very well. He had a suspicious mind, and kept asking whether an executor could steal money from the estate, and so on. I tried not to be annoyed. Tried and failed; but I don't think he noticed. We ended up making Felicity co-executor, so she could check up on my doings and co-sign everything. Would Felicity charge a fee? "I'll ask her not to," he said. I thought: good luck.

He also wanted to put in his will a long list of specific gifts to relatives, friends, neighbors, cousins, and who knows who else. "I want them all to have something that belonged to Mother. Something to remember her by." I tried to talk him out of this plan, which seemed foolish to me; but he was adamant. Why he imagined they would appreciate these pointless gifts is beyond me. I had never met his neighbor Prudence, but I doubted very much she would be thrilled with a soapstone dish in the shape of an elephant. Morris came to me with a piece of paper, listing and describing all the gewgaws he was going to leave behind, along with the names of the lucky devils who were going to inherit the stuff. The list was a yard long, I swear.

"Why don't you just leave them some money?" I said. "People appreciate money; and there are problems when you try to leave these, uh, things. In case something happens to the things, for instance."

"What's going to happen to them?"

"They might break, for instance, or you might get rid of them."

But it was no use arguing with Morris Gross. He seemed more involved with his list, than with the millions of dollars which his estate consisted of. I had to hear about each and every one of the items on the list. "There's that figurine, it's a shepherdess, it's blue and white. Mother had it on the end-table, in her bedroom. Felicity once told me, she really liked it. She said it was beautiful. So I want her to have it; it'll remind her of her dear grandma. And there's a throw rug, in the kitchen, it's from Turkey or someplace like that. Afghanistan, I don't know. I want Sebastian to have that. He told me once he likes rugs. I shouldn't do it, he's got such a fresh mouth on him, but I don't want to leave him out. And Martha's daughter, Tracy, the one that lives in Trenton, New Jersey, I don't see her much, but she sent me the nicest card last Christmas, I was thinking, what could Tracy have, and I decided, maybe Mother's collection of thimbles. My nephew, Boyd, I can't figure out what to give him, so maybe I'll let him have my wristwatch, the Rolex." And on and on.

I dutifully followed his orders. I drafted the will for him. This was about a year before he died. The will was not terribly complicated. It contained the list of gewgaws, then a gift of some $10,000 to Dr. Melrose Percival ("for his faithful service to me and my dear departed mother"), and a gift to a cleaning lady named Rosa; the rest was divided up among the rest of the family, as we had discussed. I suggested, as I usually do with clients, that I keep the original, I have a safe deposit box for that purpose; but he refused. "I'll take care of it myself," he said.

Of course, hardly had the ink on his signature dried when Morris began calling to make changes—in the list of gewgaws, as I had feared all along. "I have a cleaning service, they come in on Saturday, and one of them, a clumsy oaf, doesn't speak a word of English, he dropped the figurine, it broke into a thousand pieces. Damn fools. But I better give Felicity something else. I told the men, that it was a valuable antique, and I wanted them to pay for it."

"Did they?"

"Not a penny. They absolutely refused, the boss, they call him Pablo, he was downright insolent. I fired them on the spot."

That was one incident. Then Tracy failed to send a Christmas card, and he found out from Anna that she had been in town, to visit some friends and to go to a wedding in Cupertino; and she never bothered to call her Uncle Morris. That did it for Tracy. She forfeited the collection of thimbles. That went to a cousin who lived in Tucson, Arizona. Why he chose her for this marvelous gift of 35 thimbles, I have no idea. To be sure, some of the thimbles were antiques, he said. Morris thought they had some value. "I was thinking of taking them on that TV program, 'Antiques Roadshow.' Mother loved that program. People bring things on the show, you think they're junk, and they turn out to be worth a fortune."

Felicity got a lacquerware plate, with a picture of the Queen of England on it, on the occasion of her silver Jubilee. "Mother got that at a yard sale, for practically nothing. Mother adored it. The Queen looks so young there."

I made all these changes, in the form of a codicil. Coward that I am, I never charged Morris for this work. I had a feeling he would argue over the bill, and it was worth the small amount of money not to put up with this aggravation.

It may be cold-blooded, but I figured: when he dies, I can charge a reasonable amount. Of course I had no idea he would be dead so soon. Life is funny that way.

2

Time went by—maybe a year—and then, out of the blue, Morris Gross called me again. He said he needed to change his will, and could he come see me? Of course he could. I thought: oh God, it'll be the thimbles and the soapstone sculpture all over again.

But it wasn't that at all. "I need a whole new will," he said.

"Whatever you want, Morris," I said. We fixed a time to get together. "Tomorrow, Morris? I'm free in the late morning."

"What about the afternoon? There's a show I like to watch at eleven."

Anything for a client. At any rate, for a client as rich as Morris Gross. He came in at four o'clock.

"I want to leave everything to charity," he said. "Everything. I want to get rid of the old will."

"That's easy to do, Morris," I said. "You can just tear it up, for instance. You're the one who has it; so just pull it out of the drawer, or wherever you have it, and get rid of it."

"I don't have it. I mean, not at home," he said. "I put it in the safe deposit box. Mother had a box at Wells Fargo. Now it's mine. She had a diamond bracelet, she never wore it, she kept it in the box. With other stuff. Insurance policies. I put the will there. I didn't want anybody sneaking around the house and reading it."

I told him that was the right thing to do. And I explained to him, if we made out a new will, it would revoke the old will, automatically, because we would say so; and in any event, if we disposed of everything in the new will, the old one wouldn't matter. But still, I said, it's a good idea to tear the old will up.

"Can I ask you though, why you want to do this? Of course you have a perfect right," I said. "But if I understand you—and of course, we didn't talk about the details yet, but, I mean, if you say, you want to leave everything to charity, well, that means, your sisters, the family, they wouldn't get anything. And, as I say, you can certainly do that, no question, but I do want to ask you, why?"

He cleared his throat. "You may not know this, Frank," he said, "but I had a massive heart attack. Last June."

"I'm sorry to hear that, Morris."

"Massive," he said. "I was near the house. I was supposed to go to the dentist. I go every six months, they clean my teeth. I got dizzy, suddenly. I think it was near University Avenue. I must have fainted, I was lying on the ground, somebody found me, they called an ambulance, paramedics, they rushed me to the hospital, I don't remember a thing about it. I opened my eyes, I saw all these doctors, men in white coats, they looked worried, and then I blacked out again. . . . Frank, I was clinically dead. Frank: I was *actually* dead. I crossed over to the other side. And then they brought me back."

I wasn't sure I understood. "The other side?"

"Heaven. Whatever you want to call it. I was really there. Honest to God. At first, I couldn't believe it. I thought: where am I? Then I realized, I'm there, I'm in heaven. It's a beautiful place, so quiet, so peaceful. Like a huge garden, full of flowers. Especially roses. Mother loved roses. There were roses everywhere. Red roses, yellow roses. I felt like I was floating. But there was a path, through the garden, through the roses. It was as if a voice was telling me where to go. And I saw my brother Charlie there. Charlie! My dead brother, Charlie. I couldn't help crying when I saw him, but he told me not to cry, he was happy, he said, Morris, I'm happy here; I'm at peace. Oh, Charlie, I said, I'm so glad. I was worried about you. And then, the strangest thing happened. I saw my dear mother. . . .

"There she was, as close to me as I'm close to you. I wanted to hug her, but you don't do that in heaven, I mean, people look like they have bodies, but they actually don't. Oh, I can't tell you how I felt. I said, Mother, Mother, I knew I'd see you someday. She looked young, well, not *really* young, but not the way she looked at the end. She had snow-white hair, but she looked healthy. She had been all skin and bones. I thought, they must feed people better, up here. If they eat. I wondered about that, later on. I never found out. Anyway, there was Mother, and she called my name: 'Morris.' But there was a funny look on her face. I asked her, Mother, Mother dear, aren't you happy here? You're with Charlie, here. And Charlie is happy. And it's so nice here, so clean, the air is so good, and the flowers are so pretty. But she said no, Morris, no, I'm not happy. My spirit is troubled, she said. I said, your spirit is troubled? Why, Mother? Because of the way I died, she said. It was actually murder."

That certainly caught my attention. Of course, I had been wondering, why is he telling me this story? He must have imagined the whole thing. At least it proves he has an imagination. This is the first clue I had to any such thing. But then, the word "murder"—that jarred me, as you can imagine.

"Did you say 'murder,' Morris?"

"That's what Mother said. And I said, but Mother, you were old, you were sick, don't you remember? You had congestive heart failure, and there was something about the kidneys, remember what the doctor said, Dr. Percival, and then, you died in your sleep, all peaceful like. . . . And Dr. Percival, he signed the death certificate, and we had that lovely funeral, remember all the flowers, I hope you don't think I spent too much on them, but they were so beautiful, and remember the nice things the reverend said about you, and the neighbors, a lot of them were there, and I got you a beautiful coffin, not the most expensive one, I knew you wouldn't want that, but a nice one, not too gaudy; it was mahogany, and inside all soft, white velvet; and it was on sale, Mother; and remember, cousin Alice flew in all the way from Houston, she's got terrible arthritis, but she came anyway, to pay her respects, don't you remember, Mother?

"That doesn't matter, Morris, she said. I was old, I was sick; yes, but it wasn't my time yet. No. I consider it murder,

Morris. Cold-blooded murder. And that's what's troubling my spirit here. I can't be satisfied. I said, but Mother, the flowers, the beauty, it's heaven, you can feel God's spirit all around you. But she shook her head. There's no peace for me here, she said. It was a crime, what was done to me; and crime mustn't pay. You understand that, don't you, Morris? And I said, yes Mother. I had to ask her, Mother, you say it was murder, but why do you say that? She said, I have my reasons. I said, Mother dear, you were unconscious at the end, it was a coma, you had a heart attack—that's what Dr. Percival said, and he was there. But when I said this, she laughed, Frank. She laughed and laughed. I can't tell you how painful it was, to hear my mother laugh that way. She said, of course I know why and how it happened; there are no secrets up here. She was angry, I could tell. She said I want revenge. I said, but Mother, this is heaven, people don't think about revenge. She said, yes they do. Anyway, I do."

He stopped and looked at me. I felt, frankly, embarrassed. The man was serious about this ridiculous story. Totally serious.

He mopped his forehead with a handkerchief. "Mother said it again: there are no secrets up here, Morris, you understand that, don't you? Justice wasn't done, she said, and that's why my spirit is troubled. I said, oh Mother! Please, I can't stand that, seeing you like this. I began to cry, like a baby. Honestly, I did."

I didn't know what to say. I asked him: "Did she, your mother I mean, did she tell you what happened? Did she say who it was, who killed her? I mean, when you say 'murder,' that implies a murderer, after all."

"Frank," he said, "remember, she knew everything, because there's no secrets, no, not up in heaven. It's like ... it's like being in a movie. Everything is transparent, if you put your hand out, it goes right through people. I'll bet they could walk through walls. She knew everything, too. And you can see through people's minds, their souls. I can't explain it. There's something in the air, it's like a humming noise, it's sweet, not loud, it's a kind of music. Maybe it's harps. I think it was harps. Anyway, everything becomes so clear. But Frank, don't ask me for more details, it's between Mother and me. It's our secret."

"Yes, Morris," I said. "I can understand that. Still, if you know who killed her maybe you should tell somebody."

"Tell somebody?"

"The police," I said, "they could investigate. If there really was a crime; if somebody murdered your mother."

"No, I won't go to the police," he said.

"Because they won't believe you?" I said, feebly.

"Oh, no, not that . . . they don't have to know where I got my information. It's between you and me. I'm only telling you, because it has to do with my will. And you're my attorney. They can't make you tell, can they, Frank?"

"No, no, Morris, they can't."

"I'm telling you, because it explains why I'm doing what I'm doing. I hope you believe me. I know it's not the usual thing. But I'm not the first person to go to the other side, and then come back. It happens. I read about some little boy who went to heaven, and came back. So it can happen. And it happened to me."

I had to lie. A little white lie. Clients are clients. "Morris, I know you mean what you say. I'm not in a position to judge. There are more things in heaven and earth, Horatio," I started to say, but I forgot the rest of the quote, I knew it was Shakespeare, but I couldn't recall where. Morris asked "who's Horatio," in a suspicious tone of voice. I said, "It's nobody, Morris. Just a quote from Shakespeare. I mean, strange things *can* happen, I know that."

"If I close my eyes, I can see the whole thing," he said, mopping his bald spot again with his handkerchief. "Like it was yesterday. It was so vivid. I can see the whole scene. But I have to be careful, Frank. I have to figure out what to do. . . . I have to figure out, what Mother would want. That's the important thing."

"Of course," I said.

"That's why I came here. I have to change the will. It's wrong, the way it is now. My dear mother's money. . . . I need to make sure we do right by the money. . . . It's blood money. . . ."

I wondered why he used this expression. I had a sudden, chilling thought. Could it be because the murderer, the mysterious killer, was one of the beneficiaries of his estate? And that he was disinheriting that person, which was only natural, because they had committed this crime? But then why disinherit the rest of the family? And could he be right about his mother's death? An old, old lady? I wondered what this Dr. Percival would say. Of course I couldn't ask him.

"Anyway," he said, "somebody who . . . was responsible for Mother's death . . . he couldn't inherit her money, isn't that the case?"

"That's true," I said. "That's in the Probate Code. Plain and simple. If you murder somebody, you can't inherit any money. But that person, he could inherit *your* money, Morris. There's no problem there."

"But it's really Mother's money," he said. "That's where it came from."

"I understand," I said. "And you're quite right. Morally, it's your mother's money. But legally speaking, it's your money, now. So that's not an issue."

He nodded his head. This tidbit of legal news seemed to calm him. "Let me finish the story, Frank. There I was," he said, "in heaven. And I knew it, I was aware. . . . I was conscious of everything. It was so calm, so peaceful, as I said . . . And then, suddenly, it ended; and it was like the screen went blank, you know? And I opened my eyes, and I thought, where am I now? Am I in the other place? It seemed all dark and funny. And I heard a voice asking me something, but I couldn't answer. I couldn't see anything. Then I fell asleep I think; and when I woke up, I realized, I'm in a hospital, and there were these doctors, asking me all sorts of questions, and I had needles and tubes, I was in a bed, and. . . . But that's not the point, Frank. I gradually realized, I'm back on the earth. They sent me back."

"They?"

"Whoever. I don't know. God? Maybe Mother's spirit. I wasn't in heaven any more. And I didn't say anything to the doctors. But I kept thinking and thinking. It troubled me more and more: why? I mean, I was there, I was up in heaven, I was dead, you have to believe me, Frank. So why did they send me back? Back here I mean. They can do anything, up there, and they must have mended my poor body, and sent me down here again. They don't do that for most people. Most people, when they're dead, they stay dead. Why did they do it for me? So there has to be a reason. I was there already, I was on the other side, why couldn't I stay? That's the question I'm torturing myself with . . . and I come up with this answer: it's in order to make amends, Frank. That has to be the reason."

I nodded my head and tried to look solemn. All kinds of thoughts were racing around in my mind. I wanted his business badly. An estate of this sort, a large estate; if I eventually handled it, I could charge an extremely nice fee. I didn't wish Morris ill. I meant to be a good lawyer for him, for his estate. An ethical lawyer. That's me. But I kept thinking about money. Celia thinks the kitchen needs remodeling; and that's a major project, major amounts of money. I've been resisting; the kitchen looks perfectly OK to me. She disagrees.

Of course, I didn't believe a word of his ridiculous story. But it raised a legal issue. An issue of competence. If he cuts the whole family out, and if somebody challenges the will, and they know about this story. . . . Well, I could imagine the argument they could make: the man wasn't completely right upstairs, he was suffering from what is called in the law an "insane delusion;" and the will might be vulnerable to attack.

Will contests are actually quite rare. To be perfectly honest, I've never really handled one. I've written dozens of wills, handled dozens of estates; but never a genuine will contest. A number of times, somebody threatened to contest a will; but they either gave up, or we settled out of court. This argument, insane delusion, it's a last resort, and it doesn't often win. I remember something I read about somewhere: this man, married man, suddenly decided his daughter was really an alien from outer space, he said he wasn't her father, and that he saw her with another alien, who had taken the form of a vacuum cleaner, and she was having sex every night with the vacuum cleaner. Naturally, he cut her out of his will entirely. Why would you leave money to a daughter who was fornicating with a vacuum cleaner? The daughter won that case. I couldn't remember if it was an actual case, or something I read about in one of those magazines you see, as you wait in line at the supermarket.

Some of the actual cases in the law reports were almost as ridiculous. Men who had illusions that their wives were unfaithful, or who believed Martians were sending messages to their molars. Still, you couldn't predict how these cases would turn out. Some of these wills actually survived in court.

In this case, if relatives got wind of Morris's weird story, it might make a difference. I wondered who else he had told it to. I couldn't ask, though. And I did wonder whether a court would consider this story evidence that he had, well, a loose screw. On the other hand, people might actually believe him. After all, as Morris himself mentioned, there was this little boy, I forget his name, who told a similar story; he was four years old, and went up to heaven, and there he saw his great grandmother or something like that, and saw things he couldn't have known about; and he and his father made a best-selling book out of it, and God help us, there was a movie, too. I looked at a web site later, which discussed the book, and the issue about whether it was authentic or not. There were zillions of comments. A few of them made disparaging remarks, but the vast majority came from believers. In fact, they were bitterly critical of anybody who doubted what this wonderful little boy had recounted, they found his story heart-warming, evidence of the goodness of God and so forth and so on. I mean, religion is religion; but there has to be a limit. Like this man who found the word "God" inside a tomato; the story was, he sliced it open, and the seeds inside spelled out the word God. He thought it was evidence of divine providence or something. I found this story on the internet.

People believe what they want to believe. I have trouble with miraculous tomatoes. Why would God put a message inside a tomato?

This is a deeply religious country. That would be something in his favor. Judges don't like to call a person insane on the basis of sincere religious beliefs. It looks bad in the newspapers. I was sure I could construct a strong case for Morris, anyway. The fact that he was careful with money, and seemed disgustingly normal, in business, in daily affairs: that could be documented, and it would very likely be a winning strategy. At least I think so.

In any event, Morris and I had a talk about the new will. "Nothing to the family," he said. "Not a penny."

He did say he wanted to leave $1,000 to Rosa, a cleaning lady. "She came every Thursday, rain or shine," he said. "And she was good to Mother. She even helped her go to the bathroom, when Mother was so sick. This Rosa, she had a hard life. Her husband left her, went back to El Salvador or someplace, and she had five children, two of them twins, I don't know how she managed."

"And your mother was fond of her, I suppose."

He looked embarrassed. "Actually, not. Mother . . . she was a wonderful woman, you know, but she had her blind spots. She even hit Rosa once, with her cane, after the woman spilled cranberry juice on the rug. I said, Mother, maybe you shouldn't do that. She said, 'I'll do whatever I want to, she's lucky to have a job at all, her and her people, they come here and they take advantage, and she's such an oaf, she doesn't even speak English, after all these years.' That was Mother. She had strong opinions. She was honest to the core. I didn't say anything to her, about Rosa, after that. I feel she was a bit unfair. That's why I'd like Rosa to have a little something. When I'm not here anymore."

"She's still working for you?"

Again he looked embarrassed. "Actually, I let her go, I didn't need her, and she cost too much, $10 an hour, and she was clumsy. It wasn't just the cranberry juice. . . . She burnt one of my shirts, when she was ironing. Enough was enough. I hired a cleaning service. I gave Rosa $50 and told her not to come any more. But if she outlives me, well, she'll get this money."

Unfortunately, he didn't know Rosa's last name, or her address. "We always paid cash. Maybe she still works for my neighbor, Mrs. Whetstone. She might know the last name. And where she lives. A phone number. I'd ask her, but, well, that neighbor, we don't get along." I said I would do it. He wanted to leave the bulk of his estate to some organization "that does research on arthritis. Mother had terrible arthritis. Her fingers were all curled up, they looked awful. Like claws. She really suffered. Arthritis, it's a curse. Find out what's the best organization, one that doesn't waste money. Mother taught me, never give money to those charities that call you on the phone and pester you, or the ones that send you free things, they're just spending your hard-earned money. She gave something to one of those disease things, I can't remember, maybe it was diabetes, or Parkinson's disease, and they send her a tote bag, and she said, they're not getting another penny out of me. If they can waste money on tote bags, they aren't doing their job."

Morris wanted me to be his executor, and lawyer for the estate, and I agreed. We talked about whether he wanted to leave his money outright to this arthritis organization. He was dubious. "Suppose they waste the money?" I suggested some sort of trust, and he liked the idea. "Let Mel run it for me. Mel—that's Dr. Percival. His first name is Melrose. He can be in charge. Would that cost more money?" I explained to him that if Dr. Percival acted as trustee, he would be entitled to charge a fee. Morris didn't like the idea of a fee. "I mean, he's a doctor, isn't he? He's supposed to care about people who are suffering, isn't he?" I gently suggested that serving as a trustee wasn't like taking care of patients, and that it could be a lot of work, so that it was unreasonable to ask him to serve without pay. In the end he agreed to a modest fee, "if it's OK with Mel."

I was busy with other clients the next few days, but I did manage to begin work on Morris's will. I called up his neighbor Mrs. Whetstone. I told her I was Morris's lawyer, and she said, "What? Is he suing me?"

"No, nothing like that," I said.

"He's a horrible man," she said. "What on earth does he want from me?"

I explained, after she calmed down, that I just wanted information about Rosa. "Oh, her? I fired her," she said. "I felt sorry for her, but she was totally incompetent. I've got Cristina now. Lovely woman, totally reliable." But Mrs. Whetstone did know Rosa's full name; and she even had the number of her cell phone, and something of an address, "if she's still there."

Then I called Dr. Percival, and explained that I was working on Morris's will. He seemed very surprised. "A new will? Why?" Of course, I couldn't tell him. But I explained that Morris wanted to set up some sort of medical research foundation, and would he, Melrose Percival, act as trustee. "What would be my role?" he said. "Morris always wants something for nothing." I explained the arrangement as best I could. He grumbled, but then he agreed to the terms I had worked out with Morris. "What a guy," he said. "But I'll do it."

When I had all the information I needed, I finished a draft of the will. I called Morris and I said, "Morris, I have the will ready. You need to come in and take a look at it. If it's what you want, well, then we can sign it then and there. Or I can come to your place. Your choice."

"Oh, thank you, Frank," he said. "But can we wait a bit? I'm going on a trip. I'll be gone for a week or so. Maybe a bit more."

"Sure, Morris, no rush. Why don't I send you a copy, a draft, you know, you can look at it when you feel like it."

"Naw, I don't think so," he said. But I insisted. What was the harm? He agreed, reluctantly—I wondered why he was reluctant. The next day, I put the draft in an envelope, and mailed it to Morris. It probably got to him in a day or so.

The week went by. Frankly, I put Morris out of my mind. I had other things to think about, other clients, other matters. My client who owned a car wash was getting a divorce; I don't do divorces myself, but I was giving him advice. I had two other trusts to draft, and one of them was tricky. Ten days went by in fact. It was a Wednesday evening, I remember that clearly. Felicity Gross was on the phone. I had met her once before. And I had talked to her about Morris's will, since she was going to be co-executor. Now she sounded distraught.

"Felicity, what's the matter?" I asked her. That's when she told me about the murder. You can imagine how I felt. Shock. Disbelief. I asked for details, but Felicity knew nothing. It was all very strange.

3

The story was in the local Palo Alto newspaper, the very next day. This is one of those free newspapers, that survives, I suppose, on ads. I don't live in Palo Alto, I live in San Mateo, so normally, I don't read that newspaper. I don't even read the free newspaper in my own town. I mean, I'm a good citizen, I vote in all elections, but I can't work up an interest in bond issues, plans to widen the sidewalks, or whether a high school basketball team wins or loses. I'm not trying to find a lost pet, I'm not in the market for a used car or a new house, so why read the darn thing?

This was a different situation. I had to drive to Palo Alto on client business, and I managed to get hold of the paper. I read every word of the story. The headline was: "Wealthy Man Murdered in Luxury Condo in Palo Alto." The victim, it said, was Morris Gross, age 64. The crime took place in the evening. He was shot to death. There was no trace of the murder weapon. "The deceased was a bachelor, and lived alone. The police are examining various theories. One possibility is a botched burglary, although it was not clear what, if anything, was stolen from the condominium. None of the neighbors in the building saw or heard anything unusual." The body was discovered in the morning, by the sister of the deceased, Anna G. Maltz, who had a key to the apartment. She arrived about 10:30 a.m., according to the account in the paper, "to talk about some family matters with the deceased." Ms. Maltz was the one who called the police.

A botched burglary. But somehow I knew that this was wrong. How would a burglar get in? Usually, there was a man sitting in the reception area. Not that he was much good, but I imagine the building had surveillance cameras. And why would a burglar pick this particular apartment, on the seventh floor? I don't know much about burglars, but it seemed highly unlikely.

I couldn't help thinking ... other thoughts, ridiculous thoughts. Maybe I just have a vivid imagination. Morris had told me this strange story, about going to heaven, meeting his mother, and hearing from her that someone had killed her. And Morris seemed to know more than he told me: an actual name. Could there be a connection between Morris's story and his death? According to Morris, his information came from his mother herself, up in heaven. I didn't believe that for a minute. But Morris did. He was convinced of it. However he got his information, he was sure he knew what happened to his mother. Did he act on his suspicions? Did he talk to somebody about his theory? And did the word get out. . . . Could it be that the person who killed his mother then killed him? It seemed preposterous. Ridiculous even. But I couldn't get it out of my mind.

I talked the whole thing over with Celia, after dinner. People are supposed to have warm, friendly family dinners. Ours rarely fit that description. Each of my daughters had a friend over, and they were whispering and giggling to each other the whole time, eating the pizza we had ordered and paying no attention to the grown-ups at all. Grownups come in two versions: parents and non-parents. The parents are annoying androids whose main function is to ruin their children's lives. Non-parents are simply pieces of furniture.

After the pizza, and a struggle to get the kids to clear the table, which was almost more trouble than it was worth, the four of them disappeared into the back bedrooms, for a while. The oldest of the four, a girl named Madison, with stringy red hair, turned out to have a driver's license, and a car to go with it; and around eight o'clock they all went off to get dessert. Or so they said.

Celia and I finished cleaning up, and then lapsed into our usual catatonic state in front of the television set. Nothing caught our fancy. We rejected a show that featured zombies with a hankering for human flesh; and a reality show on which people were asked to eat tarantulas. Public television, often our haven, featured a man named Dr. Alois Dorman, who was lecturing on the structure of the brain. Our own brains were too worn out from events of the day to focus on Dr. Dorman, so we were reduced to talking to each other. I decided to ask Celia for advice. This is risky business—not that she doesn't give good advice (she most certainly does). The problem is I rarely feel like taking it.

"There was story in the Palo Alto paper, about a murder. I suppose you didn't see it."

She hadn't. "Why should I, Frank? I don't even look at our own paper. It just clutters up the driveway."

"I have to show you something," I said. I looked for the paper, which I had brought home. It wasn't where I thought it would be. I found it, eventually, in a pile of papers that were about to be recycled.

She read the article. "You know this man?"

"I knew him, yes, honey. He was a wealthy guy, a bachelor, he lived in that fancy condo on Alma Street. Actually, he was my client."

"Your client, Frank? Why is it your clients all seem to get murdered?"

"Honey, that's a bit of an exaggeration, isn't it?"

"Yes . . . but still. Most lawyers, their clients don't get murdered. You, it seems to happen all the time. If I was a client of yours, I'd start to wonder."

"I didn't lose a client," I said, "I gained an estate. A pretty lucrative one, I must say."

"Maybe you killed him yourself," she said. "You knew I wanted to redo the kitchen. And I wanted a new refrigerator. A Sub Zero. They cost a fortune."

"I have an alibi," I said. "I was home with you. It happened Tuesday evening. They found him in the morning. Remember, the girls weren't here, and we ate cheese sandwiches? We went to bed early."

"That's no alibi," she said. "Nobody believes a wife. They think she's lying."

"Whatever. Anyway, this particular murder, which I didn't commit, has some awfully strange features," I said.

"Don't they all?"

"Maybe. But not as strange as this one." And I told her about Morris's story; the trip to heaven, and so on; and how I couldn't help wondering, whether his story had something to do with his death; and should I do something about it.

"Do something? What could you do?" she said.

"Well, I could talk to the police?"

"Are you out of your mind, Frank? They'll think you're as crazy as this Morris was."

"But could it really be a coincidence?" I said.

"Frank, coincidences do happen. It's a probability thing. You know, I was talking the other day with Adam Finkel, you know him, Frank."

"Of course I do, honey. He was here for dinner last year, wasn't he?"

"Yes, he's the one."

I remembered Adam vividly. He was a math teacher, at Celia's school. A very nice man, shy, maybe 40 years old. He had some sort of terrible skin condition, all bumps and lumps on his face, which made him extremely unattractive. The kids in his math class called him Frankenstein. Kids can be amazingly cruel. "What about him?"

"He knows all about probability. He has such interesting things to say, poor man. Did you know this: suppose you've got a room with thirty people in it. What are the chances that two of them have the same birthday?"

"Pretty small, I would think."

"But you're wrong," she said. "It's more than fifty-fifty. I mean, that two people in the room have the same birthday. Adam explained it to me. There's a formula, you can figure it out, but I don't remember the details."

"What does that have to do with Morris Gross?"

"Nothing," she said. "But it's about coincidences. You remember the time my cousin Chloe was here, and Patsy, the woman who moved into Molly Unger's house, she was here too? And they somehow were talking about birthdays, and it turned out they had the same birthday. Imagine that."

I remembered that evening only vaguely. Nor did I care about Chloe's birthday, or Patsy's. I still thought there was more to the Morris Gross murder than met the eye. But Celia, obviously, was having none of it.

4

It was, of course, an unusual situation for a lawyer like me. First of all, my client had been murdered. The good news was, he had a very large estate, and I would get to handle it. The bad news was, he had told me some very disturbing things. I thought I knew *why* he was murdered—the crime had something to do with his mother's death. He knew something; something about her death. He told me that. Did that knowledge kill him?

Since Morris never signed the new will, and, as far as I knew, never destroyed the old one, the old will, the will I drew up before, was presumably still valid. Under that will, Felicity and I were co-executors. In the new will, he left nothing to his family—his sisters, his nephews and nieces. In the old will, he did. Could the murderer be one of those people in his family? They certainly had a powerful motive. Had this someone also killed the old lady?

But why would anybody want to kill Bertha Gross? Maybe the same people who might want to kill Morris Gross. She left all her money to Morris, so that doesn't make sense. But maybe they didn't know that—maybe they thought she would leave money to all of them. Also: she was 94 years old. And in bad health. Were they just tired of waiting? From all I heard, she was a mean, annoying old lady; maybe somebody felt, enough is enough.

If so, how did they do it? I had this terrible itch, this curiosity, to find out more about what happened. Not about the death of Morris Gross—presumably the police would take care of that.

But the death of Bertha Gross. The police would have no interest in Bertha. Only somebody who heard Morris's cock-and-bull story about the trip to heaven would care. I made a mental note to try to learn what I could about the last days of Bertha Gross. Who would know something about it? Maybe the doctor, Melrose Percival. Did I dare talk to him about it?

I did a little checking. Dr. Melrose Percival was a member of the Palo Alto Medical Foundation, a clinic on El Camino Real. I think he also had some sort of private practice. I made another mental note: try to find some excuse to talk to the doctor. He was in "internal medicine and family practice," which meant I could see him about just about anything. I could tell him I had lower back pains. Everybody has lower back pains, at some time or other. So long as you have a lower back, you are bound to have lower back pains.

One problem was the socio-economic structure of modern medicine. My own health insurance did not give me, as far as I knew, the right simply to waltz into a clinic in Palo Alto, and ask to see Dr. Melrose Percival. I had to stick with the San Mateo Medical Group; and my primary care physician there was a certain Dr. Sydney Smuts. Not that I was really happy with Dr. Smuts. In fact, I had been thinking seriously of switching to another doctor. Sydney was no doubt fairly capable; and he had a lot of experience. I had no real complaint against him—at any rate, no medical complaint. He was a man in his 50's, tall, angular, with a grey moustache, very thin, and with a white coat (the only thing I had ever seen him in) that seemed starched to a ridiculous degree. The problem was, Sydney was totally humorless. All business. When you have annual check-ups, which I do, you have to get undressed, and you put on a gown. This gown was obviously designed by someone with a malicious sense of humor. It simply could not be worn in such a way as to cover up the parts you wanted covered; it was impossible to tie the strings together; and when the exam includes, among other humiliations, a wriggling finger up your bottom, palpating your prostate, the least you have a right to expect is a cheerful smile, and maybe a joke. Dr. Smuts, however, was impervious to humor; and when I tried some on my part, he behaved as if he was blind, deaf and dumb. He had good things to say about my prostate; but he never cracked a smile.

I could abandon Sydney Smuts; but there was no way to transfer my business to Melrose Percival, at least no way without losing my insurance coverage. Also, if I was actually going to try to get information out of Dr. Percival, I did not want him also to palpate my prostate. Somehow, the two things seemed inconsistent.

So I put off seeing Melrose Percival, and concentrated on the business at hand. The will, for one thing. I had a copy in my files; but I needed the original, which as you recall, Morris had kept. So it was either in the condo, which I doubted, or in his safe deposit box, which was a much better place, and where I had advised him to put it—unless he had destroyed it, which I had also advised him to do.

I spoke to Felicity, and asked her if she knew what bank Morris used; my guess was, he would have a safe deposit box there. She had no idea. Bank statements? Also no idea. "Uncle Morris was not the sharing type. He was suspicious, you know, he thought people were after his money. So he played it close to the chest."

I told Felicity we should meet, and we met for lunch at the Golden Dragon, a Chinese restaurant not far from my office. Felicity was a woman in her 30's I would guess; she was tall, good-looking, and had an extremely tailored look. She had dark eyes, a nice figure, and a slightly hooked nose. There was a certain wildness about her hair, but otherwise she seemed like a person in full command of herself. The wild hair was a deep black color. I suspected it was dyed. I think I mentioned that before. I wasn't sure about the dye. Celia would know at a glance whether she did or did not dye, but I was not privy to this kind of mysterious female knowledge.

We shook hands, and got down to business. She was a no-nonsense sort of woman. I wondered why she was single. In the course of the conversation, it came out that she was divorced. There had been a brief, disastrous marriage. I didn't pry into it. She told me about the family, about who was who, and what they were like. I knew some of this already, but I listened carefully. I explained to her some of the duties of an executor, or rather co-executor. She seemed keenly intelligent. She jotted down a few notes on a small, blue pad which she took out of her purse. I was relieved and encouraged by our conversation. I could see that she would be easy to work with—sensible, efficient, non-demanding.

I told her we needed to get hold of the will. I told her Morris had made the will last year, and I thought it was either in the condo, or in some sort of safe deposit box.

"I thought there was a new will."

"Really? Why did you think so?"

"Well, Uncle Morris told me. He called me on the phone. That was unusual enough. He never called any of us, as far as I know. He said, I want to talk to you about my will. That was a big surprise. He had never mentioned a word about wills or anything else before. I have to tell you, to be perfectly honest, most of us were terrifically disappointed when my grandmother died and it turned out she left almost everything to Uncle Morris. We could certainly have used the money! But that was that; we had to swallow it, there was nothing to be done."

"Everett Mills handled that estate," I said. "Did you meet with him?"

"Yes, once or twice. Grandma did leave each of us something. A few thousand dollars. That was a scandal. The woman had millions. In a way, though, it was only to be expected. None of us liked her. *Nobody* liked her, as far as I could tell. Except Morris. If he did."

"So: Morris called you, and said he wanted to talk about his will."

"As I said, that was a big surprise. You know, we never saw much of Uncle Morris. Aunt Anna invited him to her house for Thanksgiving, and for Christmas—she always had a big dinner. I think last Christmas he came; he didn't always. When he did come, he never said much. Aunt Anna tried to be nice to him, she was always saying, have some more turkey, Morris, or try this dish, or have some pie, it's your favorite, or whatever. Kind of disgusting, the way she fawned over him. He was an old skinflint, frankly, and he always thought she was simply after his money. Which frankly I think she was. I don't think I cared much, unless I'm fooling myself. Julia . . . well, I don't know. Sebastian wanted the money, he was quite open about it. But that's Sebastian. You'll meet him I guess."

"It's a lot of money," I said.

"I know that," she said. "Poor Aunt Anna. Her husband left her next to nothing, he made bad investments, and her kids need money; and then there's me and Sebastian and Julia. Thank God I don't need anything anymore, I've got a job, but Sebastian, he has student loans, and he doesn't seem to work much. I think Julia is OK. Anyway, I'm getting off the subject. There was Uncle Morris on the phone, and he said, he had changed his will, and he wanted me to know about it. I'm leaving my money to charity. I said, Uncle Morris, it's your money, you can do whatever you want. He said, that's exactly what I intend to do. I just want to warn you, so you're not disappointed."

I thought that was rather odd. "Did he tell anybody else?"

"I think he did. He called Sebastian. And he called Aunt Anna. Maybe Julia and Aunt Martha. So none of us expected anything, really. Under this new will. But, you know, he never said boo about the old will, so all this was just plain news to us."

"There is no new will," I said. "He never got around to signing it. I called him, told him it was ready, but he put it off. Said he was going on a trip."

"A trip? Where to?"

"He didn't say."

"I can't understand it. He said he was going on a trip? Uncle Morris never went anywhere in his life. He was scared to death of traveling. He was especially leery of airplanes. I said to him once, I think it was Thanksgiving, Uncle Morris, why don't you travel? You've got the money. Go to Europe. He'd never been. He said, it costs too much. I said, that's ridiculous; you've got all that money now. Just go. But he said, I'm not getting on one of those jets, they're not safe, they're up there in the sky, and there's hijackers, people with bombs. I told him, Uncle Morris, it's the safest way to travel, really. Safest thing in the world. He repeated something about bombers, terrorists, and I said, Uncle Morris, that happens once in a blue moon. Really. He said, so you do it—it's not for me. The man was allergic to travel."

"Are you sure?"

"He was my uncle, wasn't he? Yes, I'm sure."

"Well, there's a first time for everything. Maybe he changed his mind. Maybe he didn't have to fly. He could go on a cruise. To Alaska, or the Caribbean, or anywhere. Lots of people do it," I said.

"He'd never spend the money. Frank," she said, "he absolutely positively did not go on a trip. I know this for a fact. My brother Sebastian bumped into him, last week I think it was. He saw him coming out of a barber shop on Santa Cruz Avenue, in Menlo Park. I don't know why he needed a barber, Uncle Morris was bald as an egg, on top anyway. Just had these fringes around the side. But I guess bald people go to barbers, unless they're totally bald. Anyway, Sebastian said, hello Uncle Morris, how are you, Sebastian can be charming, but as it happens, Sebastian was in a big hurry, for something or other, anyway, he didn't stop and talk. What would you talk about with that man, anyway? But there you are. You must have misheard him. There was no trip."

I hadn't misheard—that was certain. Morris Gross had lied to me, but why? Or had he planned a trip and then cancelled it for some reason? It was certainly peculiar behavior.

We agreed to meet her at the condo, where we could look for the will or for any valuable papers, things that pertained to the estate. The condo was in a tall building of luxury apartments, which was, as I said, on Alma Street, not far from downtown Palo Alto.

Felicity explained that all of the apartments in the building were condos, "and very expensive ones, too. If you wanted to buy one today. . . . Never mind; you can't afford it."

The apartment, of course, was a crime scene; and the police had been in possession, but by this time this was no longer the case. Still, it took some doing to get permission to enter the apartment. Felicity and I were presumably going to be co-executors, but we had no court order yet (we needed the will). We had to get past a large, lumpish man in a uniform, who sat in the lobby of the building. He grumbled, and seemed unwilling to help us, but he did take us to the manager, Mrs. Hortense Leopold, a rather officious woman, who looked at us suspiciously, until Felicity identified herself as Morris's niece, and I told her we two represented the estate. She kept her frosty manner, but at least she knew we weren't nosy reporters or other undesirables.

She was, I would say, around fifty years old, with hair dyed some strange color never seen in the natural world; it also looked as if she used generous amounts of hair spray. She was wearing more costume jewelry than I would have recommended; she had rings on every one of her fingers. Too much makeup, too. Her office was small and cluttered. On her desk was a picture of Mrs. Leopold, with her arm around an extremely fat man, who I imagine was her husband, and who had a silly grin on his face.

"Terrible, terrible," she said, shaking her head. "Not in my life could I imagine such a thing. In my building! I had a migraine, for hours, after they told me. I could barely move. The shock! And it was so very upsetting. Police all over the building, and the questions they asked! The people who live here, they want peace and quiet. We have only the finest residents, you understand. Stanford professors; investors, business people; we have two Nobel Prize winners, yes, two of them. We check everybody carefully before we let them buy, we turn people down, believe me; and then, imagine, something like this."

"Do you think this was a break-in?" I asked.

She really didn't answer. She clearly didn't want to answer. "We have surveillance cameras," she said. "The police have the film . . . I really can't comment. . . . That very day, we were going to show one of the apartments, it's part of an estate, it's on the fourth floor, the one with the south exposure, we don't advertise, it's all word of mouth. A lovely old woman lived there, she was the widow of an executive, with one of the very biggest companies; she had a maid, it was just the two of them in the apartment. She died a few weeks ago. I can't tell you who was going to look at the apartment, it's all confidential. You would recognize the name. We have famous people here, and of course they want privacy, they do not want any kind of scandal. Well, of course, when all this happened, the people who were going to look at 4B, they simply canceled. It's so distressing. I'm just the manager, you know; the owners are Glom and Gloster; they have some of the finest properties in the whole Bay Area. Everything first-class. There's never been anything like this, it's so awful. . . . And Mr. Gross, well, I can't imagine why anybody would want to kill him."

Of course, though I had asked the question, I knew the answer which she did not give: this was surely in no way a break-in. I desperately wanted to see what was on the surveillance cameras, but that was never going to happen. Maybe Morris had a visitor, and maybe that was captured on film. Or was it somebody in the building? Maybe one of the Nobel Prize winners decided to do away with Morris Gross. For whatever reason. I wondered: has anybody with a Nobel Prize ever committed a murder?

"I can't tell you how much it upset me," she said. "It gave me an actual migraine. I saw flashing lights in front of my eyes. Mrs. Applebaum, in 9A, she said to me, Hortense, are you ill? I never saw you like that. I told her about the migraine. Her husband is a brain surgeon, by the way. He was written up in the San Francisco Chronicle. He's the finest in the whole Bay area. His patients, only top people. One of those sheiks once flew here from some part of Arabia, just to consult him. Now he's retired."

Subversive thoughts kept entering my mind, as Mrs. Leopold went on and on about how exclusive the building was, and what wonderful residents she had. Surely she had some sort of master key. *She* could have killed Morris Gross. Maybe she did it in collaboration with a Nobel Prize winner. The motive? Maybe no motive. Just for the thrill of it. After you win the Nobel Prize, what else is left for you to do?

She was still talking, and I wasn't actually listening. I nodded my head respectfully. I needed her cooperation, and I wanted to avoid giving her yet another migraine. My own head was beginning to throb.

5

Hortense Leopold, despite her migraine, insisted on coming with us. I suppose she thought we were likely to run off with the silver. She ceremoniously opened the door, let us in, and marched in right after us.

The apartment was large and roomy. I'll spare you a description. The furniture was plush, deeply upholstered, old-fashioned but not old; and clearly somewhat expensive. The apartment had a wonderful view—well, as wonderful as one could have in Palo Alto, California, as I think I said. There was a living room, and a kind of family room, with the immense television set and the two Lazy-Boy chairs right in front of it, his and hers. Here was where Morris and his mother had spent countless afternoons, watching soap operas; and countless evenings, watching quiz shows.

In every room, on every mantelpiece, and on the coffee table, were the various gewgaws that Morris loved to list in his will. I made a mental note to check them against the lists; but of course now was not the time.

There was nothing, in the end, of enormous interest in the apartment. Later on, of course, we would have to come back and decide what to do with the furniture, the clothes, the television set, and the other objects in the condo. But for now, we were looking for bank statements, safe deposit keys, and any important documents we might find. And we were at least partially successful. In a small sitting room, Morris had some sort of desk; and in the top drawer we did find statements from Wells Fargo; and a little envelope, inside of which we found a key, which looked very much like a safe deposit key. Shortly afterwards we left.

What we did *not* find, curiously enough, was the most recent will. Or rather, the draft of it that I had sent Morris. Of course, I knew that Morris never came in to my office to sign the will; he told me that peculiar story about a trip, using that as an excuse. But I thought I would at least find the draft I had sent him. No such thing. Nor did we find the older will, which presumably was still in effect—unless he had torn it up. I suspected it was in the safe deposit box.

There was no will yet, and no probate process; but I arranged to get court permission for Felicity, as the niece of the late Morris Gross, to get into his safe deposit box where, we assumed, we would find the will. Under the beady eye of a bank official, we had the box opened. Inside was a strange collection of ancient documents, mostly belonging to his late mother, including her marriage certificate, and a package of letters to her from her husband, wrapped in blue ribbon. Love letters, believe it or not. From what I had heard about the late Bertha Gross, it was hard to think of her as anybody's love object. But apparently her husband thought otherwise, at least he did when he was courting her. Maybe he changed his mind later on.

I felt like an intruder reading these letters, and they have nothing to do with our story; I tied them up with the ribbon again, and put them back in the box. Felicity had read them too. "It's a miracle, Frank," she said. "The miracle of life. My grandfather actually loved her. They even had sex—of course I knew that; after all, they had four children. But the idea of Grandma having sex, if you knew her, I mean, it's almost obscene."

"Did you know your grandfather?"

"Only vaguely. I was ten years old when he died. Seemed like a nice man. He used to give me candy."

The letters, of course, were a side show. The other contents of the box were more important. There was an old-fashioned diamond ring, with a big and probably valuable stone. There were some ancient stock certificates, from companies that had long since moved to electronic blips. And, most significantly, an envelope which I recognized, because it had my office logo on it. Inside was the Last Will of Morris Gross. It was signed and witnessed and looked in good shape.

But this was itself a bit of a puzzle. This was the old will—the one he didn't want any longer. It certainly no longer had anything to do with Morris's wishes. He could have torn it up. He didn't. Instead, it was the draft of the *new* will that was missing. Where had that gone to? And why?

I should add, too, that we also found, in the safe deposit box, an insurance policy, on the life of Morris Gross. For a cool million dollars. Payable to his estate.

* * *

Curioser and curioser, as the phrase goes. So much about Morris Gross, his life and death, were curious. Puzzles, inconsistencies. Especially, of course, who killed him and why. But I couldn't spend all my time speculating. I had work to do, including work on Morris's estate. I filed the will dutifully in the county courthouse; and I had the will admitted to probate. That made me the executor, along with Felicity, and we had to manage the estate. We had to gather up the assets, transfer them into our names as executors, and do whatever needed to be done. I won't bore you with details.

I was sitting in my office one morning, soon after the will had been probated, when I had a phone call from a man who identified himself as Everett Mills. I knew the name: he had been Morris Gross's lawyer, and he handled the estate of Morris's mother. I vaguely recall meeting Mills once or twice, in connection with another estate, but that had been years before. I remembered that I didn't particularly care for him, but I couldn't remember why. Mills was about my age, maybe a little bit older. He practiced in Palo Alto, where he had an office in some downtown building. He had the same sort of legal practice I did.

We made small talk, and then Mills got to the point. "I'm calling about Morris Gross. I presume, from what I've been told, that you're the lawyer for the estate. Am I right about that?"

"Yes, you are," I said.

"Morris was, at one time, one of my clients. But you know that. He executed a will in my office. I assume it's been revoked. I have a copy of his older will, can I assume that it's not valid anymore?"

"That's right, Everett. There's a new will. It's been filed and probated." I could have added that the fee was going to be mine, not his. But that would have been rude. We lawyers have to get used to disappointments. I represented a wealthy woman, for years, Cornelia Slaughter; drafted wills for her, charged very little, and was as nice to her as I could possibly be. Then she died, and her daughter called me and said she had a cousin who was a lawyer—did I mind terribly if he acted as lawyer for the estate? Of course, I minded, but I had to go along. I couldn't say no. She had a right to do what she did. Life is like that.

"One thing, though. Gross owed me money. For professional services. You know I handled his mother's estate. I've been sending him bills, and he just ignored them. He was a terrible miser. But I guess you know that."

"Listen, Everett, I believe you. I knew Morris too. But I'll need some documentation. Can you do that for me, Everett?"

"Of course. No problem."

Morris's estate would pay the money; better and quicker, I thought, than Morris would have paid in his lifetime. That was the end of our conversation, as far as legitimate business was concerned. I should have hung up the phone, then and there. I could hear Celia's calm, sensible voice telling me to put down the phone and go about my affairs. But I didn't listen to that calm, sensible voice.

"Everett: can we have lunch some time? There are some things I need to talk to you about."

"What sort of things?"

"Oh, it's a long story, I hate to do it over the phone. It's . . . it's about the estate of Bertha Gross, which you handled."

He seemed puzzled and perturbed. He would have been even more perturbed if he had known what I was really after: whatever I could learn about the death of Bertha Gross. It was unlikely he could tell me much, but I had to start someplace.

I was one of the few people who knew, or suspected, that Morris's death was not the only mystery. There was Bertha's death as well.

We agreed to meet in a couple of days, in Palo Alto, in an Italian restaurant on University Avenue, which is the main street of Palo Alto, if the town is entitled to one, which it probably isn't. The whole city reeks of money—high-tech money, venture capital money, engineering money; there are upscale restaurants, and less upscale but trendy places to eat—specializing in hummus or in Vietnamese fusion, whatever that is; and of course a Starbuck's on every block, and in every one of these coffee houses, graduate students from Stanford sit sucking on their lattes and diddling with a laptop computer; they wear flipflops and T-shirts, and they dream, I suppose, of the killer app that is going to make them a fortune. Or they are budding IP lawyers; or unhatched MBA's, eager to start a hedge fund or to make huge amounts of money in derivatives and other mysterious financial things. Are any of these earnest young men—and they are mostly men—studying Shakespeare? Or the fall of the Roman Empire? I doubt it. But maybe I'm being unfair.

Everett looked older than I remembered; he's short, somewhat bowlegged, with a tiny, sharp nose, and rather beady eyes. Nobody would call him handsome. On the other hand, he was always well dressed—coat and tie, white shirt, well-polished shoes. With him, when I entered the restaurant, was a young man, in his 20's I would say. He was wearing the uniform of his age-group: T-shirt, blue jeans, flip-flops. He had a gold cross around his neck.

"This is my son, Johnny," Everett said. Johnny grunted some sort of acknowledgement. Unlike his father, he was thin; he had the same bad nose, but somehow it looked better on him. Maybe Everett had simply aged poorly. "He's my one and only," Everett added. "He's living with me, right now. He got his certificate from Foothill College . . . but right now, he's sort of between situations."

I was somewhat disappointed that Everett had brought his son along. My ulterior motive was to find out more about the late Bertha Gross; and I really didn't need a third person in the conversation. I decided to go ahead with my questions anyway. First there was some dull lawyerly small talk, followed by serious study of the menu.

"I can't do tomato sauce," Everett said. "It gives me heartburn."

He was also allergic to pesto. And nuts. "Does this dish have nuts in it?" he asked the waiter, pointing to something on the menu.

His son said, "Dad, you're being obnoxious. Stop asking so many questions."

"Nuts could kill me," Everett said. "I could go into shock."

Johnny shrugged his shoulders, as if to say, go into shock, see if I care. Was this going to be an unpleasant lunch? I tried to make more small talk. It was a monologue. Everett was terribly quiet. I said something about the fog coming in early. Then suddenly he said: "Why are we here, Frank? What's this all about? You brought me here to talk about the weather?"

"No . . . of course not."

"Then what? You're going to pay up, aren't you? The money that little shit, Morris Gross, owed me. This isn't about that, is it?"

"No. Everett, you'll be paid, I guarantee it. To be honest, I wanted to ask you about Bertha Gross, not Morris."

"What about her? She's dead and gone. She took her time dying. I had to kiss up to that horrible woman for years and years and years. Eons it seemed like. I had to say, yes Mrs. Gross, of course Mrs. Gross; she was cheap, miserable, a colossal pain in the ass, but I held out, because I wanted the estate. And I got it, finally. I thought I would have to kill her to get it." Johnny snickered at this.

"That's my old man," Johnny said.

Interesting expression: "I thought I would have to kill her." I couldn't help wondering, maybe he *did* kill her. I made a mental note to put him down on the list of suspects.

"Oh, I earned that money," Everett said. "Not only waiting for the old biddy to die, but dealing with Morris Gross. That was something, let me tell you. Makes you want to believe in karma, reincarnation, and that sort of crap. That woman's soul went straight into her sonny-boy. Maybe he was always like that. Cheap and demanding. Probably from birth. But I didn't have to deal with him, as long as *she* was alive."

"But you knew him," I said.

"More or less. I was at the condo maybe a dozen times. Bertha wouldn't come to the office; I had to go to her. Not that she couldn't go out of the house; she just didn't want to accommodate me or anybody else. She was paying me, so she thought she could treat me like a slave. So I went to the condo. He was always there. Two of a kind. But he hardly opened his mouth. And she ordered him around, it was disgusting, Morris, do this, Morris, bring me this or that. And all he said was, yes Mother."

"Were you surprised that she died?" I asked, feebly.

"Surprised? Yes and no. For God's sake, she was 94; but, yes, I was surprised. I thought she was too mean to die. She was full of piss and vinegar, right up to the day she died. I mean, I was there."

"What do you mean, you were there?"

He hesitated; as if he had said something he hadn't really meant to say. "I mean, at her condo."

"When she died?"

"For God's sake, no. But I was there that evening—the evening she died. Well, there was no piss and vinegar that evening. About a week before she died, she called me up and, the old crone, she said she wanted me to come out, and right away; I said, I'm busy, can't this wait, and she said, no it can't wait, and I'll get somebody else if you're not willing to do your job, blah blah. She was more than usually obnoxious. I said, I have to be in court, and she said, well, there's too many lawyers in the world anyway, and I'm sure some of them are hungry for my business. So I agreed to come out there, around dinner time. She was in their dining room, with a sour look on her face, and her lapdog, Morris, was there, and her doctor, he was there too. Percival, Dr. Percival. I guess he was a guest; anyway, they were eating dinner. She didn't even offer me a cup of coffee."

"What did she want?"

"Why do you need to know, Frank? What is this? Anyway, it's confidential. Lawyer-client privilege and all that."

I said, "she's dead, Everett."

"Oh, what the hell. She wanted to change her will. The other two, they were sitting there, they didn't say a word. She was that kind of client, always changing her will. Not that she wanted to pay me each time; no, she thought I should do it for nothing or maybe she wanted a package deal. Or something like the airlines, you know, frequent flyer benefits—ten wills and you get the eleventh one free. Anyway, I took notes on what she wanted. She was a sadistic old thing. She started in, how worthless her relatives were, only Morris, he was the only one, the others didn't care, they pretended, but they never came by, that sort of thing, blah blah. Well, if she was my mother, I wouldn't come by either. Anyway: she wanted to leave almost everything to Morris, a few small gifts here and there, but the bulk of it to Morris. He didn't say boo. I said, fine, if that's what you want. So I went back to the office, and I drafted the will for her. She wanted it right away, of course, and I had to drag my weary bones out to the house, and I took Johnny with me, and one of the associates in the office, and she signed the will, and they witnessed it, and that was that."

"And that was the last will. . . ."

"Well: yes. But then, the day before she died, she called me up again She said, she needed to make a change. In the will. It was terribly important. With her, for God's sake, everything was 'terribly important.' She was so wrapped up in herself. It's like, as she got older, and got more shriveled up, more arthritic, somehow everything dried up but a small, little turd-like ego. Anyway, she said I had to come out there, that very day."

"What did she want? I mean, what did she want to do about her will?"

"I never found out. When I got there, it was after dinner, eight o'clock I think; anyway, the doctor, he was there, and Morris was sitting in the corner, pale as a ghost, and there was also a couple of other people, her granddaughter Felicity, and her daughter Anna, and another man, didn't know him, never found out who he was. Or what they were doing there. And the doctor; did I mention the doctor? Melrose what's-his-name. He was there. And I said, Mrs. Gross called me, and she wanted to see me. And the doctor said, she's not feeling well, she's lying down. I said, oh. And I waited a bit. Then he said, really, I think you'd better come back in the morning. She's not going to be able to see you. They were all sitting around there. Weird, I thought. And I was annoyed, because I had wasted my time. But I could see, it was no use. So I went away. That night she died. I guess she had been taken ill, and that's why they were all there. But nobody told me anything. And of course, since she was dead, I never found out what she wanted. She said, terribly important. But who knows? People like her, they think every toe-nail is important."

My mind was whirling about. I could picture the scene. The old lady was going to die that night: had somebody in that room done her in? I mean, not Morris, of course. Felicity? The doctor? Anna? Or the other man, whoever he was? I had to ask Felicity about this scene. But how? What excuse would I use?

"Aren't you listening, Frank?" he said, with a sharp tone in his voice. I had been lost in thought. I guess it was obvious.

"Every word, Everett," I said.

"I bet. Anyway, did I tell you what you wanted to know? Listen, Frank, you've got some ulterior motive. Don't lie to me. You know what? I don't give a crap what it is, or why you care about the old lady and her last night on earth. Just tell me you're going to pay my bill. I worked hard on that old lady's estate, and I want to be paid for it."

I made the promise. After all, he did deserve to be paid. He had done the work. Morris was stingy; but now Morris was dead; and I knew Felicity wouldn't make any trouble. So the bill would be paid, as it should be.

I called her at her office the next day. She worked at Stanford, as a researcher. I had asked her once what she did. "We do research on old people," she said. "Nutrition issues. Old people don't eat right. We have this project, trying to improve their diets. I had this one subject, he was 82 years old, he ate nothing but peanut butter and jelly sandwiches. Oh yes, his wife was vegan. I had my hands full; not just with them. We've got a protocol we have to follow ... we've got a government grant, NIH grant.... You know, it's not easy to get old people to join these studies, you have to pay them, of course, and they're cranky and they're sick half the time. But I love the job, Frank."

I told Felicity about Everett's bill, and explained why we really had to pay it. She agreed immediately. She was obviously going to be easy to work with. Then came the hard part: "Felicity," I said, "the night your grandmother died, you were at the condo. You and your aunt Anna."

"I was. How did you know? And why do you care?"

"Oh, nothing," I said. "Idle curiosity. Everett Mills was telling me about it. He said he came over to see your grandmother, but she was too sick to see him."

"So? That's right. She wasn't feeling well. That's what they told me too, when I came over. I had this crazy idea, I'd interview my grandmother. For my study. Find out what she ate. For all I knew, she subsisted entirely on human blood. She had that kind of personality. But I never saw her. I must have come shortly before Everett. They told me she was lying down."

"Who else was there?"

"Why are you asking?"

Why indeed. "Well, she was planning on changing her will, and, uh, that could have had an impact on Morris's estate."

I realized immediately how feeble this was. Felicity was no fool. "I don't see the connection. She never changed anything, the woman died in her sleep."

"Felicity, humor me, OK? Everett said your aunt Anna was there, and the doctor; and another man. Who was that?"

"I'm trying to remember. Let me see: it was Sheppard Schwartz. He was Grandma's accountant."

"Her accountant? What was he doing there?"

"I have no idea. You could ask him. "

Asking Sheppard Schwartz was no problem at all. He was also Morris's accountant. I called him, and told him I wanted to touch base with him. Later, we got together at my office. He was a man in his 50's, thin, with gray hair, and a very precise way of speaking. He was not the sort of man you want to have a beer with, although, come to think of it, there isn't anybody I want to have a beer with; but I had a good feeling about his honesty and competence. We talked about the estate, a lot of the nuts and bolts, the assets, the tax consequences, and so on. He had everything under total control. And then I shifted subtly—I think it was subtle—to a discussion of Bertha's estate. "You were her accountant, no? And I understand you were there the night she, uh, died."

He looked at me with a somewhat puzzled air. But he said yes, he was. I asked: "Forgive me for asking, Sheppard, but why were you there? Was there some special reason?"

He said: "Frank, I actually don't know. Bertha was a very demanding woman, but a fair one, an honest one; and when she said she wanted to see me, and she wanted me to come to her place, I agreed, because I felt, she must have had a darn good reason. She said it was something she couldn't discuss on the phone."

"And did you discuss it with her?"

"No, I didn't. When I got there, her daughter was there, Anna, and Morris of course, and Dr. Percival; and they said she wasn't feeling well. I said, I'm sorry to hear that. I waited for a while, and then I went home."

"So you never found out."

"No, I never did. She died in her sleep that night. I imagine the thing had something to do with her investments. Or with her insurance. She used to talk to me about her insurance, ask advice. I told her, Bertha, I'm not an insurance agent. You should see an insurance agent. At any rate, I'll never know, will I?"

I was intrigued. A picture was forming in my mind. The old woman wanted to do something, something she considered important. Change her will? Change her investment portfolio? She called her lawyer, she called her accountant. But she never even got to talk to them about it. Very conveniently, she died that night. I was becoming quite convinced that there must be something to Morris's peculiar story, about his visit to heaven.

Not that I believed in the heavenly visitation; but the message—that somebody killed his mother—that seemed not quite so ridiculous. Did somebody do her in, to prevent her from talking to her lawyer and her accountant? And why? And who could it be? Anna? The doctor? Somebody else? Maybe somebody poisoned her, but the poison didn't work right away. I know nothing about poisons. Maybe the guilty person was somebody who visited her earlier in the day. My mind was whirling madly about.

"After Bertha died, I worked with Morris, as you know," he said. "Bertha's affairs were in apple-pie order. Well-managed; I helped her with a wealth management company, and the results were more than satisfactory. I did the same with Morris. Morris knew very little about investments; basically, we simply left things as they were. With one exception. I talked to Morris, of course, about his own estate plans. He wanted to buy a big insurance policy, payable to the estate. I told him, he didn't need insurance, but he insisted. He said, Mother believed in insurance, she had a big policy, and she told him, if anything happened to her, she wanted him to get himself insured. . . ."

I was barely listening. The people there that night, at Bertha Gross's, they have to be suspects. She must have been either smothered or poisoned. Whichever way, the doctor could have covered it up. Any other mode of killing her would have been much too obvious. I assume that Morris had no idea what was going on. Not then. But if Everett and Schwartz were telling the truth, I have to leave them off the list of suspects; they had no real opportunity; they never even saw the woman. Unless they came before, earlier in the day. . . . But wouldn't Morris have noticed?

But why am I even *thinking* about this? The only evidence I have that somebody killed Bertha Gross, is this weird heaven story. . . .

It could be the reflection of some subliminal thing. . . . Had something happened to put this idea into Morris's mind?

OK: whether somebody killed Bertha, that's unknown. And maybe unlikely. But somebody definitely killed Morris.

"Poor Morris," I said, just to make conversation. "It was so sudden. And so violent."

Sheppard shook his head, and looked very solemn. "I can't imagine why anybody would want to kill Morris. It must have been an intruder. You can't be too careful these days. So much crime. I tell you, I was shocked, really shocked when I heard the news. In fact, I knew nothing about it for a full two days. I was out of town, at a convention—an accountancy meeting, convention, whatever you want to call it. In Akron, Ohio. Nobody told me until I got back."

Well, at least that cuts him off the list of suspects. Not that I suspected him, really. He sat quietly in the chair, wiping the lenses of his glasses with a small square piece of cloth. I couldn't imagine him killing anybody. My brother-in-law Steven is an accountant, in Philadelphia. I can't imagine him killing anybody either. Sheppard reminds me of him. He's a good man, Steven. Accountants are people, after all. Like lawyers. We're definitely people.

I guess I have to look elsewhere for my murderer.

6

I was busy the next few days with other clients; and I didn't have much time to think about Morris Gross and his mysterious death.

On a bright, sunny day, Felicity called me. She said she'd like me to come meet the family. "I think it's important; at least I think you should meet the ones that are getting the money. You know, when I told them, it was a big shock. They thought Morris had disinherited them."

"I wonder why he told them that."

"I don't know. Really. I haven't got a clue what got into him, the last weeks or so. I mean, like this business of taking a trip: a complete lie. I just don't understand it. Anyway: I told you he spoke to me about not leaving me any money; turns out he spoke to all of us, Julia, Sebastian, Aunt Anna; called us, individually, on the telephone. Pretty blunt about it, too. He even called Aunt Martha. Anyway, what he said was, Grandma wanted the money to go to charity, or something like that, and he was honoring her wishes, and anyway, we didn't have a right to it, which of course we didn't. And now it turns out, we're getting the money after all. Another big surprise."

I felt like saying, he never had a chance to sign the will. Somebody killed him. But I thought that would be extremely indelicate, since the people who benefitted from the murder were the very people she had mentioned. I wondered if they had alibis. You had to exclude Aunt Martha; she was far, far away. But the rest of them?

We were going to meet in Aunt Anna's place. She lived in

Mountain View, just off Castro Street, the main street of the town, a bustling and lively street lined with Asian restaurants, Chinese, Japanese, Vietnamese, even Mongolian. Aunt Anna owned a modest two-level condo, attached to the building next door. A nice neighborhood. Solidly middle-class. When I arrived, in the evening, Anna greeted me, and welcomed me in. She was there, in the living-room, along with two younger people who I assumed (correctly) to be Julia and Sebastian. Somewhat to my surprise, Dr. Melrose Percival was also there.

Anna was a tall, gray-haired woman, with a fussy manner. She resembled Felicity. I imagine she might have been quite attractive when she was younger. She had her hair drawn back, in a kind of bun, which made her look a bit severe. Julia, her niece, was a rather plain young woman, with very little make-up, and dishwater hair. Dr. Percival was a middle-aged man, with a slim white moustache, long, bony fingers, and slightly stooped shoulders. The liveliest of the bunch was Sebastian Gross. Sebastian resembled his sister Julia, at least superficially. He was tall and lanky, with dark blonde hair; he talked incessantly, and constantly interrupted people. When he shook my hand he said, "So this is the great detective." I started to protest; but Sebastian, as I soon discovered, never seemed to listen to what other people had to say. At first I was irritated, but then I got over it. Maybe it was the way he looked, his somehow open face, his big pale blue eyes; he seemed frank, innocent, likeable—and certainly, irrepressible.

"You'll get used to Sebastian," Felicity said.

Once in a while, his aunt would say, "Do be quiet, Sebastian, let other people talk." He never paid the slightest attention.

The conversation was about family, about estate matters, and sometimes it veered off onto other subjects, almost at random. Julia almost never spoke. I learned a lot about family history, at least in bits and pieces. I wondered why Dr. Percival was there; and Aunt Anna seemed to read my mind. "Melrose is almost one of the family," she said. "He was so good to my dear mother. I'll never forget his kindness, never."

"She's talking about our grandmother," Sebastian said.

"She was really something else. Most people love their grand-mothers, grandmothers are sweet old things that give kids presents on their birthdays. Lucky kids. Our grandma was the Wicked Witch of the West."

"Sebastian, really; your grandmother, show some respect," Anna said.

"She left every penny to Uncle Morris," he said. "And I wasted my time, kissing up to her. I could have saved myself the trouble."

"Oh, Sebastian," Anna said. "Mother did what she wanted. Uncle Morris took care of her, and that was his reward. Yes, I could have used the money myself. For my children, I mean. But it's not for us to complain. She did what she wanted to do. She had a hard life. I miss her terribly."

"Hard life?" he said. "What was so hard about it? She had her sonny-boy, Uncle Morris, he waited on her hand and foot, and she was filthy rich. She could have had anything she want-ed. God knows why she wanted him. Hey, with her money, she could have had anybody she wanted. I mean, not when she was 90. She could have hired some young stud. At least at one time. She was a widow for ages. But no, instead, she had Uncle Morris."

"Sebastian, how *can* you say such awful things," Anna said. But plainly he *could* say such things, and he did, probably all the time. I wondered if she really minded. I cleared my throat, and brought the conversation back to estate matters. I said, "as you know, you're the beneficiaries of Morris Gross's estate, together with his sister, Martha, who lives in Fort Lee, New Jersey, I understand. I'm told she's in bad health."

"Practically crippled with arthritis," Anna said. "My poor sister. She couldn't even come out for the funeral. I spoke to her on the phone, and she was terribly broken up, losing her brother. First Charlie, then Morris."

"I don't believe she gave a damn about Morris," Sebastian said. "And the money will do wonders for her arthritis, I'm willing to bet."

I kept steering the conversation to the will and the estate. "As you all know," I said, "Morris Gross seems to have been a bit undecided about exactly what he wanted to do with his estate. I'm told he called all of you, and said, he was going to change his will, leave the whole thing to charity; but he never did, and no matter what he said or wanted, it's the will that counts."

"I went to see him, the very day he died," Anna said. "I told him, he was my brother, and the money was his, and he should do with it whatever he wants. I said I had no hard feelings."

"Oh come on, Aunt Anna," Sebastian said. "You wanted the money. That's why you went, to try to talk him into it. It's OK, I don't blame you, I wanted money too. But don't say you had no hard feelings. We all had hard feelings. How could we not? Anyway, he was lying to us. Maybe all the time. I wonder why. I guess he was seriously weird."

I thought I saw a way to get into the subject I really wanted to discuss: Bertha Gross. I said to Anna: "It must be a comfort to you, Mrs. Maltz, that you had a chance to see your brother so soon before he died. I understand you saw your mother, too, just before she died."

Anna gave me a piercing look. "How did you know that?"

"I'm sorry, is that a delicate subject? I didn't mean to be offensive."

She wiped away a tear. Whether a sincere tear, or a histrionic tear, I can't be sure. "It's so painful to think about. I know she was old, very old, and so frail, the poor dear, but still. . . . Yes, I was there. If I had known, I was never going to see my dear mother again. I came up to the apartment. Morris was there, and Melrose. They said Mother wasn't well, she was lying down. I peeked in on her, she was in bed, eyes closed, I know this sounds crazy, but I think she was smiling. My dear, dear mother. It was the last time I ever saw her. That's why it's so . . . etched in my mind."

"Was she sick? You said the doctor was there?"

"Melrose is a friend of the family. That's why he's here. Melrose was there for some medical reason, isn't that the case?"

"Not really," he said.

"You said she was unwell, Morris said you told her to lie

down. And then, poor thing, she died in her sleep. So peaceful-
ly. That's what I'd want for myself."

Melrose Percival opened his mouth, as if he wanted to say
something; then obviously thought better of it. I would have
loved to hear *his* account of Bertha's last day on earth.

Sebastian said: "Aunt Anna, I know she was your mother
and all that, but if you saw her smiling, that would be a first.
She was as sour as a dill pickle."

"Sebastian, that's really enough," she said. "Your own
grandmother."

"Auntie dear, I didn't pick her as a grandmother. You
know, people have two grandmothers. There was Grandma
Tilden, too. She was a real sweetheart. Nothing like Grandma
Gross. She sent us a chocolate turkey once, for Thanksgiving. It
was really big, I mean, not as big as a real turkey, but it must
have weighed five pounds. We loved it. Ate till we got sick.
Unfortunately, Grandma Tilden lived in Kansas City. You have
to wonder why people live in those places. I know, there are two
cities with that name. She was in the Kansas one. Anyway, she
died ten years ago."

"Your grandmother loved you," Anna said.

"She had a funny way of showing it," he said. "Always carp-
ing and complaining. You know, I said to her once, Grandma,
you're always complaining. I mean, get a life. I told her what I
thought. I always do."

That much was obvious. Aunt Anna looked shocked. Or
tried to look shocked. I could see that neither Julia nor Felicity
was paying much attention.

"Did you see her much, Sebastian?" I asked. "I mean, your
grandmother." Of course, I didn't want anybody to know my
suspicions. They all thought Bertha died a natural death. Morris had a different idea. Maybe it was crazy; but somehow I
believed he must be right. People in heaven don't lie. I don't
mean that seriously; I don't think Morris Gross ever died and
went to heaven and came back. But something planted that
idea in his mind.

If it was murder, who could be guilty? Anna and the doctor
were the most obvious suspects; they were there that night, and

something strange seemed to be going on. But of course, if she was poisoned, it could have happened earlier in the day; I could imagine somebody coming over, visiting, and slipping something into her tea, or her medicine, or even into a glass of water. I wanted to know who had been there that day, but I couldn't for the life of me think of a reason for asking.

"Did I see much of Grandma?" Sebastian said. "Not if I could help it. But . . . well, not entirely. She was rich; and I thought, why shouldn't she leave money to her beloved grandchildren? So I would pay her a visit once in a while. Butter her up. I should have known better. She was unbutterupable. Actually, my current girlfriend lives in the building. Abby Whetstone. Her mother lives across the way from Uncle Morris. Millicent Whetstone. They didn't like each other."

I had finished my business; I had gotten to know the family, and there was nothing more to be gained from the visit. Aunt Anna served coffee and cake; I stayed a bit, and then said that I had to be going. Sebastian excused himself too. We went out together. "Can I give you a lift?" I asked. But he had his bicycle nearby. "I like to use my bike. Good exercise," he said. I got in my car and drove home.

I had learned some things; but they didn't add up to much.

Celia was waiting for me when I came home. She had made some sort of stew, which she reheated in the microwave. We sat and talked. She said, "Frank, tell me you're not getting yourself enmeshed in this business. This murder. Your client, Morris Gross."

"Me, dear?"

"Well, who else? Tell me: *are* you?"

I told her what she wanted to hear. What I didn't say was this: no, I'm leaving the death of Morris Gross to the police. It's the death of Bertha Gross that fascinates me.

Was I telling a lie to my wife? Is it a lie when you just don't mention something? I told myself, in a lawyerly way, no, it was definitely not a lie; it's not a lie to leave something out, leave something unsaid. That was the lawyer in me. Celia, who had never gone to law school, might have had a different opinion.

7

It was time for Felicity and me to go back to the apartment. There were so many details to take care of. I met Felicity outside the building. I was a few minutes early, and I had a chance to walk around and look at the grounds. A man in overalls was watering the plants, a riot of blue, orange, and pink flowers, set among smooth gray rocks and stones.

In the entrance hall, with its snazzy chrome furniture, an old man, in some sort of uniform, sat behind the desk, daydreaming. I was dying to ask him if he had worked there long; how many people had his wonderful job; who of them had been there when Bertha Gross lived (and died) in the building; and if he knew who had come to visit her the day she died. But of course he would have absolutely no memory of any such thing.

We had less trouble with the manager this time; she gave us a key without any fuss. We went up in the elevator to the seventh floor. There were only two apartments on the floor. One had been Morris's, the other belonged to Mrs. Whetstone. Both of them were doubles, that is, normally there were four apartments to a floor, but both the Gross and the Whetstone apartments consisted of two apartments remodeled into one.

The interior was a bit musty; it smelled of death, or was I just imagining this? "It's depressing, Frank," Felicity said. "You know, a man's dead, but somehow, he's all over the place, if you know what I mean. His shoes, his underwear, bills from the gas company. . . . Paper clips. Uncle Morris had a lifetime supply of paper clips. I never saw so many paper clips. And there was still stuff left over from Grandma. Even some of her clothes, in one of the closets. Morris more or less left her bedroom the way it was."

On this second visit, we had scheduled more time to look around; and to assess what had to be done. I found the condo in some ways quite astonishing. The old woman had been extremely rich; and after her death, so was Morris. I assume Morris never had much to say about furnishing and decorating; maybe it was old man Gross whose taste was reflected in the condo. I assume too that the furniture was expensive; multi-millionaires don't get their furniture from the Salvation Army. Nonetheless, the furniture struck me as old-fashioned, and extremely ugly. In the main living-room, over a gigantic green sofa, there was a landscape painting, a scene with purplish mountains, and three waterfalls. I hated it. "It's a Frescobaldi painting," Felicity said. "Late nineteenth century. Do you like it?"

"Not really. Who is Frescobaldi? Sounds Italian."

"Some American painter, he just took an Italian name. He was not exactly Rembrandt. I think the old man bought it, my grandfather. It's worth a lot, actually. Some people love his work. There's no accounting for taste. My grandmother couldn't care less about art, she was only interested in money. Bought all of her clothes on sale. She thought only a fool paid full price for anything."

There was a kind of family room, with a giant television screen. I thought about mother and son, spending evening after evening, slumped down in those huge, ungainly chairs, watching television until it was time to go to bed; I imagined old Bertha nodding off, beginning to snore, then waking up with a jolt and telling Morris to get to bed.

"Most of the people in this building are old," Felicity said. "Old and rich. I've never seen any young people, young couples, or people with kids, unless they were visiting some relative. It's kind of an old people's home, only not officially."

We went to work. Felicity was more concerned with simply getting the lay of the land. There was a lot to be done. The clothes to be gotten rid of. The condo would have to be sold. Furniture. Whatever odds and ends were around the apartment. We would need an appraiser, to put a dollar value on the art work, if you could call it that, and on other things—dishes, silver. Felicity had a notebook, and she went around, looking from room to room, making notes on what she saw.

Morris had turned a small room, originally a bedroom no doubt, into a sort of study. Or maybe it was already a study when Bertha was alive. There were a few chairs, and a large wooden desk; also a file cabinet. I began going through the drawers. There were papers of various sorts, letters, bills, invoices, and the like. Everything was in total disarray. There seemed to be no sort of system. I took a look at the file cabinet. I opened the drawers. They were even more disorderly—files lying on their side, helter-skelter.

"Was it this way the last time we were here?" I asked Felicity.

"We didn't look very closely," she said.

"Was your uncle neat?"

"Uncle Morris? He was positively obsessive."

I showed her the file cabinet, and the desk drawers. Felicity seemed upset. She said: "Frank, this isn't right. Something's wrong here. Somebody's been through these files, messed them up. Uncle Morris never did this. He wouldn't. And unless I'm crazy, this isn't the way they were the last time we were here."

"Who could have done it?" I asked. But I knew the answer. Not exactly who: but whoever killed him was very likely the person who rummaged about, looking for something. Maybe on the night he died, or since then perhaps? Somebody had been in here: that was clear. But looking for what? Or could it have been the police?

As I looked around, I remembered Morris's long list of "specific bequests," the technical term that describes the list of gewgaws he mentioned in the will. I had noticed some of them casually the first time we had been in the condo. Now I was sorry I hadn't brought the list with me. I remembered some of the items, and I had the impression that some of them were missing. Where was the soapstone elephant, for example? Or the Meissen statuette of a shepherdess with her gaggle of little sheep? These were two that I remembered; and they seemed to be gone. Could this have been a robbery after all? Were some of these gimcracks valuable? I mean, *really* valuable?

After a while, I found the job tiresome. So did Felicity. "It's depressing," she said, sitting down in the living room, on one of the sofas. "So much to do. And so sad. If I believed in ghosts, I'd think that Uncle Morris was here, haunting the place. I'll have to find out how to get rid of the clothes. Donate them to charity or whatever."

"And the papers? I don't mean bills and so on; but letters, and I also noticed a photo album; what do you want to do with them?"

She said. "None of us care, except Aunt Anna. She said she wanted to see whatever there was. Pictures especially. That photo album: it's something Grandma kept."

"It'll be a lot of work, cleaning out the place, I suppose."

"There's this nosy neighbor, Prudence Goldfinch, she lived right downstairs, she offered to help out; she said she was a friend, that she would miss him, which I think is unlikely, and she told me how much she loved my dear grandmother, which can't be true either: nobody could love her. Well, I guess Uncle Morris loved his mother, if he loved anybody. They had a lot in common. Stingy, misanthropic. But Grandma had a powerful personality—you have to give her that. I don't think Morris had much of anything. Maybe she squeezed everything out of him."

I asked her how familiar she was with the apartment.

"I wasn't here that much," she said. "Especially after Grandma died. It does look as if somebody was looking for something, in the drawers. I can't believe it was Morris who was so sloppy. So maybe it was a break-in after all. Maybe he kept a lot of cash around; some people do. The banks are paying so little these days, you might as well keep your money under a mattress."

I told her it seemed very unlikely. A break-in on the seventh floor of the building? And there was, after all, no sign of a break-in. "And when was this done? I mean, suppose somebody came here . . . they didn't necessarily break in. Maybe they had a key. Do you know who had a key to the place?"

Felicity looked at me. "Nobody," she said. Why did I think she was lying?

"And, as far as know," I said, "nothing was stolen." I said nothing about the missing gewgaws. If they were in fact missing. No point mentioning them; I would have to check the list in my office.

Felicity gave me an odd look. "I guess that's true. That nothing was stolen."

"Why do you just 'guess' it's true?"

"Aunt Anna thinks. . . . Oh, you better talk to her about it. . . . She has some crazy notion; it's so over the top I won't even mention it. "

I went back to the boring job of going through files and desk drawers, this time more carefully than before. I fully expected to find nothing. But I was wrong. In the bottom drawer of the desk, I found a sealed envelope. It was stuffed in the back of the drawer, under a pile of cords, paper clips, scissors, and staplers—as if somebody was trying to hide it. No wonder we hadn't seen it the first time. And to my utter amazement, the envelope bore the words "Last Will of Morris Gross," in a handwriting that I recognized as his. I tore it open. Inside was a single sheet of paper, plain white paper. The message on the paper was entirely handwritten. The heading was the same as on the outside of the envelope: "Last Will of Morris Gross." The text was short and sweet: "This is the last will of Morris Gross. I leave $100,000 to the charity mentioned in a will that my lawyer drafted. I leave $1,000 to Rosa Gonzalez. The rest goes to my family: one-third to each of my sisters, one third to be divided among the children of my brother Charlie. My niece Felicity to be executor. I would like Frank May to be the lawyer for the estate." It was signed: "Morris Gross." And it was dated: three days before Morris died.

"Felicity," I said, "look at this."

She read it, wide-eyed. "Is this legal?"

"Absolutely. It's what's called a holographic will. They're perfectly legal in California, so long as they're handwritten. And look at the date, Felicity. Morris did this a few days before he died."

"Frank," she said. "This is really weird. Could it be a forgery? How come we didn't see this before?"

"Well, it was easy to overlook. We weren't very thorough."

"Are you sure, Frank? Maybe it wasn't there. Maybe it's a fake, maybe somebody came and put it here."

"Felicity, that's just not very likely. Let me ask you—but I think I know the answer—did anybody in the family know about this will?"

"I don't think so. I mean, I can't be sure. I didn't know a thing about it. I can ask people. What does this mean?"

"I honestly don't know." I was totally at sea. Why would Morris Gross do this? He never signed the will I drafted, the one that disinherited everybody. But why? Why did he change his mind? Actually, since he never signed the new will, the old one was presumably still valid; he didn't need this holograph. But maybe Morris didn't know that. He was, to put it mildly, less than astute with regard to legal affairs.

Apparently, he told nobody about the holograph. It was a deep, dark secret. On the other hand, he told the whole family about the new draft, the one he hadn't signed. They thought they were disinherited. They were wrong, of course. He never signed the draft; and indeed he went so far as to execute this holograph—which left almost all of his estate to the family, an absolute fortune. What on earth was he thinking about?

Was he afraid of something? Of somebody? Of course, I didn't know yet if this holograph was genuine. I would have to check out the handwriting. And we would have to start all over with the probate process; we would have to file this new will.

Was it possible that somebody had taken this will, and then put it back? Who could that be? Who had a key to the condo? If only I had access to the surveillance cameras; but of course I didn't, and there was no way I could go to the police with this story and see the film. I could ask the man who worked at the reception desk downstairs, but I had the feeling he basically saw nothing and remembered nothing. . . . No, there was nothing to hope for there.

Assuming the holograph was genuine: what did this do to my theory that he wanted to change his will, in order to disinherit somebody? Maybe he lied to everybody, told everybody he was leaving all his money to charity, because he didn't want some one particular person to get suspicious? And meanwhile, secretly, he made out a new will.

But the new will didn't disinherit anybody. Not anybody in the family. It was basically the same as the original will, except that it did leave out Dr. Melrose Percival. Was that significant?

Felicity was now looking in the desk drawers, pulling out bills, invoices, pieces of paper. We had gone over these lightly before; but now we were looking for things that were not quite so obvious. She said: "Wow. Frank: here's something else. A sealed letter. It says: 'For Frank May.' You better take a look at it."

I opened it up: It was addressed to "Frank May, attorney for my estate." It said: "To Frank May: in case of accident or sudden illness, I have made out a will, the kind you just write on a piece of paper. I read about this kind of will in the AARP magazine. It is in a sealed envelope, in one of the drawers of my desk. If you find this will, please notice the other document, which will be in a sealed envelope next to the will. This has on it also the words, 'for Frank May, attorney.' I want the contents of that document kept entirely secret. In this document, I have written the name of a certain person. It is my wish to exclude that person from any share in my estate whatsoever, no matter what kind of claim that person might make. Not one penny. I have very good reasons for doing this. I would like you to make sure this happens. Inside the envelope will be $1,000 in cash, as payment to you for doing what I want you to do. Morris Gross."

I showed it to Felicity. I asked her, "Do you have any idea what this is all about?"

"Not a clue, Frank. But where's that letter?"

We rummaged through the drawers, the files, we spent two hours going through every piece of paper we could find. That other letter was gone.

Somebody had taken it; that was clear. And did that person also take the holographic will—and then bring it back? My head was reeling. This was puzzle after puzzle. It occurred to me that the missing letter would give me the name of somebody he thought was responsible for his mother's death. Could it be a member of his family? But he left his money to the family. . . . There was something discordant here. If it was a family member, why not just leave that person out of the will? Why go through this rigmarole, which was legally meaningless anyway.

Legally meaningless. But Morris Gross was not a sophisticated man, not when it came to law, wills, probate, and the rest of it. He thought he had a way to prevent that person from getting his money, by some sort of lawyer trick, I suppose. And Morris obviously thought I would do this magic trick for a measly thousand dollars.

I looked at Felicity. She was sitting on the couch, and she was crying. I was shocked. She seemed so strong, normally, so impervious. A rock of Gibraltar. Now she wiped her eyes, and said, "I'm sorry, Frank . . . sorry about this. . . ."

"Felicity: don't apologize. It's a stressful situation."

"Frank," she said, "I love my family. But we're so screwed up. . . . My parents are dead, I had this horrible grandmother. . . . And now this business with Uncle Morris. . . . I don't know what to think. . . . Tell me honestly, Frank, do you think . . . maybe one of us . . . killed Uncle Morris? And who took that letter? Was that one of us too?"

I handed her a tissue. I had no answers.

8

When we had finished with the apartment, we went downstairs. In the lobby, a rather stout but handsome woman, in her late 50's I would say, came up to us. She had dyed hair; but most women do in her age bracket. She was elegantly dressed, with a strand of pearls around her neck. She said hello to Felicity, who introduced her to me. "Frank, this is Prudence Goldfinch. She lived right below Morris, on the sixth floor."

"He was a lovely man," Prudence said. "I was so saddened by the news."

"Did you know him well?" I asked her.

"Not really well. People in this building are very private. I knew his mother better. Bertha. She was a woman with a strong character. So tragic, both of them dying," she said.

Felicity thanked her for the sentiment.

"Bertha was a good woman," Prudence said. "And she had such lovely things. The pictures. And the little details. That's what makes a house beautiful—the little details. She had some little Limoges pieces, I admired them. And soapstone. I love soapstone."

"Yes," Felicity said, "Grandma liked to collect little things like that."

"If you need any help," Prudence said, "I would be so happy to help out, to be useful. I know there's tons of things to be done. When my own dear mother died, five years ago, I went through this kind of ordeal. She had a house, a small house in Redwood City, and there was no one to help me. I know how much work it is. And then, when I had cleaned everything out, I had to put the house up for sale. It was so painful, showing strangers around the house I grew up in. So . . . if there's anything I can do. . . ."

"That's kind of you," Felicity said. "I'll keep you in mind."

Afterwards, Felicity and I had coffee on University Avenue, in Palo Alto. "Who was that woman?" I asked. "I know she was a neighbor."

"I know she used to visit Grandma. She's a divorced woman, I don't think she has children. Her husband ran off with his secretary. There's rumors she has financial problems."

"Was Morris friendly with her? Or with other neighbors?"

"I don't think so. There's also Millicent Whetstone, who lives next door. Sebastian mentioned her, I think; he's dating her daughter. But she and Morris were not at all friendly."

We drank our coffee, and talked about the latest developments. I told her what had to be done, now that we had a later will. "It's not that different, in essence, from what we had before, except for the gift to the charity; otherwise, you are all still the heirs. But we do have to inform the family about these developments."

"Let me handle that," Felicity said. I was perfectly willing to let her. I think she must have done this immediately, because her Aunt Anna called me the very next day. She asked if she could come see me, and of course I said yes, and we fixed a time.

She appeared promptly. She asked a whole series of questions about the estate. "This is such a surprise. I can't imagine what my brother was thinking, why he did what he did. Telling us we wouldn't get any money, and then. . . . It's so unlike him. I do need the money, I won't lie about that. My husband made bad investments, and when my mother died, I thought I would inherit some money. . . . Does that sound callous?"

"Not at all," I said. "It's perfectly natural."

She said: "I loved my mother, but she had a will of iron, and as you know, my brother got everything, which wasn't really fair. So now, it's only justice that some of that money will come my way. Of course, I would give up every penny, every last penny, to have dear Morris back, my only brother, now that

Charlie's dead, and my sister, Martha, she isn't well, and she lives so far away. Yes. . . . The money. . . . But still, Morris dead, it's terribly upsetting, losing a brother this way."

"I understand," I said.

She said: "All of this is so surprising. And so strange. I think it was just plain mean, what he did. Telling us we wouldn't get any money. When I heard that, heard him say, he was leaving everything to charity, I thought. Morris, how could you. Charity begins at home. So, yes, I went to see him. I told him I needed money. I said, I hoped he lived a long time, but he had a duty to his family. It wasn't right of Mother to leave it all to him. It just wasn't right. I said, we were his flesh and blood, and he had a duty to help us in our troubles. I said, Morris, I wish you a long life, I hope you live to be 90, I really hope so. But right now, you have to share your good fortune with us. I mean, I deserved some of it. I know he was good to my mother, I don't begrudge him getting some of the money, maybe even most of it, the money, but why all of it? Why didn't she leave me some of it? I always wondered if Morris didn't poison her mind against me. . . . And the rest of us. Martha; so crippled with arthritis, and I think she's not well off. And poor Charlie's three children. And then, after all that, to say he wouldn't give us anything, I mean, it was just too much. I broke down and cried. But now that's over and done with. He's done the right thing. Why he lied, I'll never understand. Would it be out of place to ask how much money would be coming to me? And when? Is there . . . any way I could get an advance?"

I explained to her that first we had to get the probate process going. I tried to make clear, the various nuts and bolts of the process. Then, when I had a chance, I said, "Anna—can I call you Anna—" (she nodded her head), "your niece, Felicity, told me you thought something had been stolen, out of your brother's place. . . ."

She looked at me sharply, even angrily. "Why on earth are you asking? It's . . . a very private matter."

"I don't mean to offend you, Anna," I said. "But, uh, we have to make sure we collect all the assets of the estate and if, well, something was missing, we have to know about it. I'm sure you realize the importance."

I hate telling this kind of fib. But I do it anyway.

She seemed somewhat mollified. She said, "Oh, but it's nothing. Really nothing. Felicity dramatizes things. I should never have mentioned it to her, the silly girl. It's too ridiculous."

"But what were you referring to? Something stolen."

"Really, Frank, I'd rather not say. Well: if you insist. You see, I was there the day before, or maybe it was two days before, visiting Morris. Ever since Mother died, I wanted to make sure everything was OK. Morris was so attached to her. It was a beautiful relationship. I only wish my own children were like that. But what's the use? They have their own lives to lead. I can't complain."

Have you ever noticed that people who say "I can't complain," use the expression just before they launch into their own episode of bitter complaining?

"I have two children," she said. "And I know, they lead busy lives. My son Boyd, for instance; he works for this company, in Philadelphia, I don't know what they make exactly, something to do with computers; but he has to travel all the time. He's never home, his wife doesn't like that, but he says, Mother, what else can I do? I said to him, Boyd, why don't you come out to California more often? I never see you. He says, you know why, Mother. And I do know why. It's his mother-in-law. She dominates the family. And his wife, Karen, I don't like to criticize, but she spends money like water; and they have two children, and they go to private schools, it costs a fortune; aren't the public schools good enough where they live? And they have household help, too, a cleaning lady. Why Karen can't keep the house clean herself, I have no idea. She doesn't have a job, she just lays around the house. I said to him, Boyd, how can you afford all this? And he can't. He called me up, and he was actually crying. Mother, I'm on the verge of bankruptcy. I need money. I said, how much, and he mentioned a figure. . . . I said, Boyd, I haven't got that kind of money. This was after my mother died. So he said to me, didn't Grandma leave you money? She was so rich. I said, yes, she was a very rich woman;

but she left every penny of it to your Uncle Morris. . . . I haven't got anything; your father, God bless him, never made much money, and he invested in start-ups and hedge funds, I don't even know what those are; I've got my social security pension, but precious little else. Imagine. I had to turn down my own son."

I grunted something more or less to indicate sympathy.

"And my daughter, Cassandra," she said, "she lives in London, with this guitar player, they're not even married. I told her, my darling, you're throwing your life away with that bum; but she as much as told me to mind my own business. I said, you're my daughter, you *are* my business. I can't sleep nights thinking about the kind of life she leads. Imagine, a guitar player. In some sort of band. That kind of person, they're always on drugs, and they stay up all night, it's not a normal way to live. And to think of my daughter with that man. He has tattoos all over him. The one time I saw him, I thought, this man is disgusting, his hair was down to his shoulder, and he had an earring or something of the sort, and god knows what else. They came here on a trip. It was the first time I saw him, and I said, Cassie, never bring that man into my house again. And she laughed! She actually laughed!"

I interrupted this stream of consciousness by asking again, if anything had been stolen.

"Stolen? No; what was there to steal? Morris had nothing worth stealing in that house. Oh, they spent money, Mother spent money on furniture, she had the best, but she didn't have things people want to steal, money, jewelry, she never wore jewelry, only a strand of pearls, and it was right there in the top drawer of the dresser. I couldn't help crying my eyes out when I saw it. I thought of her, in the old days, before she was sick, in a black dress she used to wear, with those beautiful pearls. I thought, at least, I'll have the pearls. Or Martha will. But no, it went to Morris with everything else. Morris! As if he had any use for pearls. Well, never mind. No, nothing was stolen. I'm sorry I ever said anything to Felicity."

I wasn't giving up so easily. I said: "I understand. But exactly what did you say to Felicity? You did say something was stolen, didn't you?"

"I just said—oh, it's so ridiculous, it isn't worth repeating. I mean, the day I was there, I don't remember the exact date, I was talking to Morris, I was telling him about this letter I got from Cassandra, it was a terrible letter, not like the letter a daughter should write to her own mother, as if I didn't have a right to criticize, which I do, and as if I wasn't thinking only about her, which of course I was, and that awful man, Simon—his name was Simon. Imagine, he actually has a prison record. My own daughter, mixed up with a creature like that. And I was in tears, literally in tears, and I had this splitting headache, and Morris said, Anna, stop crying, and go get some aspirin, and I went to the medicine cabinet, and I didn't find any aspirin, there was something else, Aleve or Advil or one of those, I don't remember which one, and I took two of them, with some water. I get these headaches all the time. Dr. Percival says it's my nerves."

I played with a pencil. "Headaches can be awful," I said, for want of anything better.

"Well, then, this terrible thing happened, I mean, Morris getting killed, and the police were all over the place, and so on, and I went over, and they wanted to ask me questions, I was there in the condo, you can imagine how I felt. All those questions, and I said, my brother is dead, have mercy on me, and I had another headache, it was a splitting headache again, and I said, let me get some aspirin, and I went to the medicine cabinet, and. . . . Oh, it's too ridiculous. I must have been mistaken. But I thought there were a couple of things missing."

"Things missing? From the medicine cabinet? What do you mean?"

"Toothpaste. I noticed the toothpaste when I was there, you know, when I had that headache. It was right next to the Advil or whatever I took. It wasn't the usual kind, but that sort of toothpaste you use for sensitive teeth. I never understood why people do that, I suppose Morris had sensitive teeth, I said, Morris, what's wrong with your teeth? And he said, my teeth?

What is this all about? So I said, well why are you using that weird toothpaste? He said, what on earth are you talking about, and what business is it of yours what toothpaste I use. Well, I said, don't get all huffy, Morris. I'm interested in your welfare. He said, the hell you are, you're just interested in my money. So we had this nasty argument, and it was all because of that toothpaste. I left there in tears."

"And the toothpaste was missing, after he, uh, died?"

"I told you, I had another bad headache, and I was crying, I get sentimental, and poor Morris, he was my brother, after all. To think of him, dead. And that somebody killed him. It broke my heart. I was there, they were asking me questions, and like I said, I just couldn't stand it, and I said, I have this terrible headache, I have to get something out of the bathroom, and I was looking for the Advil, and I noticed, the toothpaste was gone. There was a tube of Colgate, ordinary toothpaste, mint toothpaste, you know, but the other thing, it just wasn't there."

"And you think it was stolen?"

"Oh, of course not. That's ridiculous. Why would somebody steal toothpaste. Felicity has a vivid imagination, she really does. I shouldn't have mentioned it at all. But I did. Because . . . it's a heartbreak, it really is. I know what happened. We had had this argument, and I called him and I said, Morris, we mustn't quarrel, we're brother and sister, and I wanted to make up to him, you know, I said, the doctor told me, my nerves are all shot, and he said, well, don't blame me, and I said, no, Morris, I'm not blaming you, I just want to be on good terms, that's all, we're supposed to love each other. Imagine having a fight about toothpaste. And he seemed to get all angry, and he said pardon my French, but forget the damn toothpaste. But I know it must have troubled him. Morris wasn't a bad man. And he was a family person. The way he took care of Mother. Nobody on this earth took care of their old mother the way Morris did. I hate to think what's in store for me, my kids would never do anything for me, Mother was lucky: she had Morris. My daughter-in-law Karen, what could I expect from her? And Cassandra? I'll end up in an old people's home. No, I think Morris threw the toothpaste away, and bought some regular toothpaste. Just to please me. And when I realized that he did that, and now he was dead, and he made that wonderful gesture, why, I couldn't help it, I burst into tears. I picked up that tube of Colgate and I cried and cried. I was crying all over the toothpaste. People would have thought I'm crazy, I'm clutching a tube of toothpaste and crying bitter tears, they're all over the toothpaste. I said Morris, forgive me. I know you bought this to please me."

I nodded my head. "I understand," I said.

"I'm an emotional person," she said. "I feel things, here, in my heart. It touched me. And I couldn't just keep it inside, all bottled up; so I told Felicity about it. She's someone you can talk to. But now she's repeated it, to you. She shouldn't have done that. And Sebastian knows about it too. And he's so unpredictable."

"I'm sure Felicity meant well," I said. "And . . . it was just the toothpaste, Anna? The thing that was missing."

"Well, no. Not just toothpaste. There was something else. But I'm not going to tell you what it was, it's too embarrassing."

Embarrassing things in the medicine cabinet? I could think of some definite possibilities. I made up my mind to check my own medicine cabinet, just to make sure there was nothing embarrassing to be found. I wish I knew exactly what Anna was referring to. I wanted to ask her; but I was sure she would say nothing more on the subject.

"You know, I saw him, the day he died," she said. "I went there in the early evening. I was so anxious to make amends. I really was. And, I'll be honest with you, the money business, it rankled me. Leaving everything to charity. Because that's what we thought. And I wondered, was he mad at us, was it something we did? Morris was a very private person. Maybe he took offense at something. So . . . I was there. We talked a while. He was rude to me, poor man, his last day on earth, and something must have been bothering him. I stayed only a short time. And to think, somebody came in later and . . . shot him. I can't get it out of my mind."

"You said something was bothering him?"

"Oh, I don't know. I thought so. Who knows. And I thought

I heard something, when I left, when I was in the elevator, before the door closed. Somebody going in or out. It could have been that awful Whetstone woman, she lives next door."

* * *

Afterwards, I thought about this conversation. Aunt Anna was fussy and officious, and she talked too much. But I found it hard to imagine that she killed her own brother, or killed anyone, for that matter. Still, I had to put her on the list of suspects. She had been there the day Morris died, after all. Did she have a motive? She had also been at the condo the day Bertha died. Suppose Morris knew a secret: he knew that somebody had in fact killed his mother. And suppose that person knew that Morris somehow had discovered the truth—wouldn't that person have a good reason to go after Morris?

But why had this somebody killed old Bertha? The answer was obvious: for money. Anna, for example, thought she would get some of the money. Still, if it seemed unlikely that she would kill her brother, it was even less likely that she would kill her own mother.

Who could I talk to? I had to keep quiet at home. Celia would never forgive me, if I meddled in these affairs again—I had done it once too often. Even so, Celia seemed suspicious. She had an uncanny sense, an intuition, that told her when I was interfering in something she thought I should keep away from. "Are you behaving yourself, Frank?" she asked me, after dinner.

"As always," I said.

"I asked you the other day to pick up some olives. and you forgot. And when I reminded you, you went out and got black olives, when I distinctly told you green ones."

"That's true. I forgot. But why are you bringing that up?"

"Because you behave that way when you decide to play detective. I'll never forget the fiasco with the olive oil, the time we had Adam for dinner."

I also had never forgotten it. That was in the midst of another situation, when another client had mysteriously died. I had ruined a dinner party by buying the wrong sort of olive oil.

No, Celia was not the right person to talk to. Did I dare talk to Felicity? She seemed so sensible. We were scheduled to have lunch the next day, to talk over more estate matters. We met at Jodhpur, an Indian restaurant, at her insistence; she claimed she loved Indian food. It gives me heartburn, as a matter of fact; but clients are clients.

Felicity was digging into a plate of unidentified vegetables, smothered in a lime-green curry sauce. It was the kind of sauce that would be the absolute death of me, if I dared eat it. I stuck to Indian bread, rice, and tandoori chicken. We had a pleasant, business-like conversation; and then Felicity began speaking openly to me about things that were very much on her mind. And mine.

"Frank, I can't stop thinking about this awful thing. Uncle Morris. Somebody actually killed him. It's like something out of a bad novel. And what's worse, it was somebody he knew. Aunt Anna likes to talk about a prowler, but I don't believe it for a minute. Nobody broke in. Nobody. It was somebody he let in. And nothing was stolen. Well, toothpaste, if you believe Aunt Anna."

"Somebody went through his papers," I said.

"Yes: but who? Burglars and prowlers don't do that. That makes it even worse. It was somebody who—oh, God, it seems so terrible; somebody killed Uncle Morris, and then, while the body was lying there, went through all the file drawers. And, Frank, I keep asking myself, could it be somebody in the family? One of us? Is that possible?"

"Felicity, how would I know?"

"Of course, of course. But, Frank, I hear these rumors. . . ."

"Rumors?"

"About you. You, Frank. That you have a certain skill."

"Skill?"

"At figuring things out. I heard about another situation, not exactly like this one, but still, they say you were marvelous. The police were totally baffled, but you figured things out."

Oh God. Not again. Of course, I did my best to deny any such skill to Felicity; but as is always the case, it was quite useless. In a way, I decided to give in. I said I wasn't formally involved, but that of course I was curious; the whole affair was mysterious, and very troubling, and I could understand why it was bothering Felicity. After all, she herself had to be something of a suspect. "Do we know who was there that day? I mean, the day somebody killed your Uncle Morris?"

"I have no idea," she said. "I mean I assume the police know. Don't they have surveillance cameras, and there's a kind of doorman there, or receptionist. He's asleep or reading a magazine half the time; and it's just an apartment building, you don't have to sign in and out. He could notice people, but I think he never does. You know, Frank, any of us could have been there; we're family, Uncle Morris would let us in. Still, I have to remind you, Frank, that we really didn't go there very often. He was a cranky and disagreeable man. You know that. At least the three of us, me, Julia, and Sebastian, we rarely saw him. Aunt Anna, she was different."

"Different?"

"Well, she was actually there that day," Felicity said. "I know that. Listen: Frank, I feel awful even bringing this up. Aunt Anna is wonderful, she was like a mother to us, our own mother was dead, and then our father died, too; but she's not an easy person. She's kind and generous, but she's also very demanding. Strict with us. She felt, she had failed with her own children, and she meant to be right with us. I mean, it was for our own good. Anyway, that's beside the point. I think Uncle Morris resented her. She has a way of butting into your life, that's why she can't get along with her children; Sebastian and I. . . . Well, you know Sebastian. He knows how to butter her up, and how to ignore her in a clever way, so that she doesn't even know he's ignoring her, if you know what I mean. And actually, she adores Sebastian. He has a real way with women, old, young, whatever. Sometimes I wonder how he got in our family. . . . And then there's Julia. She's quiet, passive even, but I know that she resented Aunt Anna at times. I'm sure she did."

I wasn't interested in how the three of them got along with Aunt Anna; I wanted to know more about Anna's visits to the apartment. "You said she was there that day? Did your uncle invite her, or did she go on her own?"

"On her own, I guess."

"Just a sisterly visit?"

"I doubt it," she said. "Look: I'll be honest. She was after him for money. Constantly. Not that she ever got anything out of him. I said, Aunt Anna, forget the money. It's a lost cause. We thought he would live twenty years, anyway. Oh, one other thing I should mention, she had a key to his apartment."

"He gave her a key?"

"Actually, he didn't. She had it from before. She said she needed it, to visit her mother, not that she did that very often. But after my grandmother died, she used to visit Morris once in a while, and she let herself in with the key, and he had a fit. He considered it an invasion of privacy. He said, Anna, I want to know when you're coming and when you're not coming. I don't want you barging in on me. I don't want you to have the key to this place. I want you to give me that key."

"And did she?"

"I hate to tell you, but she did and she didn't. She made a copy of the key, and then she gave him the original. He didn't know this. She could still come and go. Of course, she didn't dare use it when he was around.... I'm not saying she ever used it at all, but she had it. I think you should know that."

I liked Felicity. I trusted her. She was a sensible, intelligent woman; she seemed reliable, a woman with her feet on the ground. But I wasn't sure what she was trying to tell me. Was she accusing her aunt of murder?

9

Despite all my denials, the rumor that I was somehow the Great Detective had a way of spreading. "I tell people it's ridiculous," I said to Celia, "but they don't believe me."

"Frank, I know you," she said. "It's been—what?—twenty years that we're married. You deny it, but you deny it in a way that makes them think, he's just saying that. He's playing a game. He's being coy, and so on."

Spouses always imagine they can see right through you. Sometimes they're right.

Did my denials sound hollow? Maybe they did. The very next day I had a visit from Millicent Whetstone, Morris's neighbor. She came to my office. She was a middle-aged woman, rather fat, with a mop of hair she had dyed some sort of off-color orange, and an abundance of costume jewelry, including a necklace which looked as if it weighed a ton and was made out of semi-precious rocks, if there is such a thing. At any rate, it consisted of round, obese beads, of every conceivable color. She had a nice smile though, and she smiled and laughed a lot. She wheezed a little, when she talked; and she had a funny way of talking, almost an accent.

After she introduced herself, and I induced her to call me Frank (and agreed to call her Millicent) she launched into a little speech. "You know, I live across the corridor from where that man lived, Morris Gross. Dreadful man, by the way. Anyway, my nephew Basil is a lawyer. I was talking to him about this case. I know it's none of my business, but I thought I should talk to you. I told him what happened. How somebody came in and killed that horrible man. I'm sorry, I know, you shouldn't speak ill of the dead, but he was an awful, awful person. I can't say I'm sorry he's dead. But in the building! How terrible. I could hardly sleep, I was so frightened. I live right next door. It could have been me. I mean, if it was a burglar. But then, it wasn't a burglar, was it?"

"I don't think so," I said.

"That's what they're saying. The people in the building. They're saying, it's no burglar. The whole building is buzzing, as you can imagine. Most exciting thing that happened since the last time the power went out, and we were in the dark for simply *days*. Frankly, I enjoyed it. Well, except that the food spoiled in my freezer, the meat, and all that luscious ice cream; but maybe that was good for me. And the elevator wasn't working, and can you imagine climbing up and down seven floors? We have meetings, condo meetings, and we talked about a generator, something that would keep us going if the power went out. Anyway, that was last year's news. It's a comfort, in a way, what you say. I mean, I'm not talking about the generator, I'm talking about Morris. That it wasn't a burglar. Though that means, it was somebody he knew. Family, most likely. Anyway, my nephew, Basil, he's quite brilliant, my sister's son, he went to Harvard Law School, they say it's almost impossible to get in, but Basil did it. Now he works in San Francisco, big law firm, he makes a ton of money. He was telling me, he said, Aunt Millicent, it's the law, if you kill somebody, you can't inherit from them; that's right, isn't it?"

"Yes, it is."

"Well, it only stands to reason, doesn't it? Otherwise, people would go around killing people, just to get their money. You're wondering, why is it any of my business. Of course, it is, because of the neighbor thing. And then, my daughter, she's dating this young man, Sebastian Gross—Morris's nephew—did you know that?"

"Actually, I did."

"I said, dating. Oh my, that's such an old-fashioned word. Well, I'm old-fashioned, in a way. Now Sebastian: he's a suspect, I suppose. The whole family is. Not that Sebastian would kill anybody. He's such a dear boy. Do you know, for mother's day, he gave me this absolutely gorgeous bouquet. My own daughter wouldn't give me the time of day, but Sebastian, he's so very thoughtful. I said to Abby—that's my daughter—now, how come a perfect stranger gives me flowers, and you don't. And she said, well he's hardly a stranger, Mother dear. And don't get taken in, she says, Sebastian is out for himself, and don't think it's out of the goodness of his heart. I said, well, so what, if it means giving flowers to an old lady, I'm all for it; he can 'take me in,' as you put it, any time he likes. I mean, Sebastian is fun. We can laugh and laugh when we're together. I said, Abby, you're such a sour puss, look at Sebastian. But anyway: it's not Sebastian I'm thinking of. It's Morris's sister. Anna."

"Anna? What about her?"

"She was there. The day he died. I had gone shopping, I go to the Safeway in Menlo Park, at least once a week, I try to do all my shopping, and I had two big bags of groceries, mesh bags, you know they make you pay ten cents for a bag these days, can you imagine? Oh well, it's for conservation or something. I'm happy to cooperate, I mean, we have to do our bit, don't we? Anyway, it was late afternoon, I don't remember the exact time, and I got out of the elevator, and she was coming out of his room. Maybe he was dead already, I don't know. She's not a nice woman. I said hello, and she just glared at me."

"Did you know her personally? I mean, Anna?"

"Oh, did I ever. And I knew her husband, Boris. Before I moved to this building, I lived in another building, and Anna and Boris and their family, they lived there too. Then I got out of there, and we bought this condo; and this was just right for me, the right price, and the right location. My husband died a year later, he left me well-fixed, thank God; I tell you though, when I found out we had new neighbors, and I was going to be living next door to Anna's mother, I thought, oh this is too much. We almost decided to move out. I thought, it's my fate, wherever I go, there's this family. But this is the point I want to make. Boris, he was very conservative, awful man; he was in the NRA, always talking about the right to bear arms or that nonsense. I said to him once, what, you think you have a right to all those terrible automatic things, machine guns, god knows what else. He had three or four guns that I know of. Maybe he had more. Well, what happened to those guns? He died, and everything went to Anna, I suppose. So that means she had guns. When she came out of the door, she was carrying a big purse, the gun could have been in there."

"You think she killed her own brother?"

"Well, I know it sounds bad. . . . But somebody did. There's something wrong with that whole family. They're not nice people. Really. I mean, that man, that Morris. Nasty, stingy old man. And the old lady, I used to call her the dragon lady. I said to Abby, let's buy a voodoo doll, and stick pins in it. They're some bunch. Or were. All of them, except Sebastian. I don't know his sisters, though, I have to admit. Sebastian gave me the idea about the voodoo doll: he said he tried it once. Oh, we had a good laugh about this. Anyway, I asked him once, Sebastian, how did you become so sweet, with that bunch, that grandmother, that uncle, that aunt? He laughed. But it's true, he's different from the rest. I said, Sebastian, if I was thirty years younger, I'd want you for a boyfriend. And he said, well, Millie, nowadays, maybe that's not so unusual, anything goes, hey, maybe I should dump your daughter and have a fling with you. Oh, I tell you, we had another good laugh about that. He's got a lot of charm—and none of the others, I mean, Morris Gross, not an ounce of charm. I said, Sebastian, I don't want to say bad things about your family. He said, Millicent my love, go right ahead; I do it myself. But, you know, I don't know them, really. I only knew the old lady, and Morris, and Anna, and they were all bitter, stingy people. I know I shouldn't be gossiping, but still. . . . What was she doing there, that day? If you had seen the look on her face. And it must have been, just about that time, I mean, when he died."

"Well, did you tell this to the police?"

"The police? Oh, goodness no. I don't want to get mixed up with this thing. I saw this TV show about the police, how they frame people. Oh, no. I wanted to tell Sebastian, he's such a dear, but I was afraid to. That's why I'm telling you, I need to know what to do. They say people trust you; and that if you say something to a lawyer, his lips are sealed. Oh, and I'm so afraid that she'll find out, I mean, Anna; you can't keep anything secret any more. With these cameras and things. Not that cameras have anything to do with it, but people don't respect privacy. You really can't trust anybody these days. Or anything. No, no. I'm telling you. . . ."

"But, Millicent, what would you like me to do? I'm really not a detective."

"Oh, I don't know. I really don't. I just wanted to talk to somebody. I haven't even told my daughter. I don't want her to get mixed up in this, the whole thing is so sordid. But if that woman. . . . If she killed her brother. I mean, it's frightening, isn't it? I've kept it to myself. Well, mostly. I did tell one person. Prudence. Prudence Goldfinch. She has the apartment just underneath. I had to tell somebody, I swore her to secrecy. I told her about Anna, and she said, funny thing, I saw her too. So you see, I'm not so crazy. I told her to talk to you, but she said, no, no, I don't want to get mixed up in this, I'm helping the family out, with the apartment, she said, you know, getting rid of the stuff that was there, but other than that, no thank you."

I told her she was right about privacy. Lawyers have to keep confidential matters to themselves. I wasn't sure this rule applied to Millicent; she wasn't a client, after all. But I said it anyway.

She said, "Oh, that's such a relief. . . . But will you talk to Prudence, at least? So you know I'm telling the truth?"

I told her I believed her, I didn't need corroboration. But she insisted. "I'm having her over for coffee, please drop in, give some excuse."

I was reluctant to do this; but I finally agreed. I was also a bit curious about the layout of the Whetstone apartment. How likely was it that she could hear what was going on in the next apartment, where Morris lived?

The answer was: unlikely. There was a kind of hall, leading actually to the kitchen and a small dining room. The apartment was as large as Morris's. His condo, as I said, consisted of two apartments, joined together into one. The Whetstones had done the same. The living room faced the garden side of the apartment building; it was, I imagined, somewhat insulated from any sounds that might come from the Gross's place. Would she have heard a gunshot? I would have loved to find out if that was the case. But of course, that was simply impossible. In the first place I don't have a gun. I know the NRA thinks we should all have guns, absolutely everybody, including cloistered nuns, kindergarten teachers, and circus clowns; and all kids over the age of eight; but I have no desire to oblige the NRA. In the second place, I don't think either the police or Felicity or anybody else would appreciate it, if I performed that kind of stunt.

Millicent greeted me at the door and kissed me on both cheeks. "I'm so glad you could come, Frank, you're an absolute dear. Come meet Prudence."

Prudence Goldfinch was already there, sitting on a sofa in the living room. She was wearing the same sort of severe black dress she had on the first time I saw her, and the pearl necklace, which might or might not have been genuine. Celia would have known in an instant. I suppose that any woman who lived in the building was assumed to be able to afford real pearls; but you can never tell.

"This is Frank May," Millicent said. "I told you about him."

Prudence looked at me. "We've met," she said. She had a kind of sharp eye—I don't quite know how to describe it; she gave the impression that she was studying me, judging me, assessing me. It made me vaguely uncomfortable. I sat down on a long sofa, upholstered in some kind of nubby orange material. In front of me was a coffee table, with bowls of fruit, and an assortment of pastries. "Frank, try the apricot tart," Millicent said. "Do you take tea or coffee?"

I opted for coffee. The apricot tart was, in fact, delicious, although I found it impossible to avoid smearing some of it on my shirt. Prudence took nothing except a single blue grape from the bowl of fruit. "You live downstairs, Mrs. Goldfinch, is that correct?"

"It's Ms. Goldfinch," she said. "I'm divorced, and I took back my name."

I noticed she failed to invite me to call her Prudence. But I let that pass. "Terrible thing," I said. "The murder, I mean."

"This building is full of busybodies," she said. "They positively revel in it. I think it's disgusting."

"Oh, Prudence," Millie said, "it's only human. And aren't you helping out, in the apartment, you know, with the clothes and so on? I know Felicity really appreciates your help."

"I want to help," she said. "But gossip is another thing. I hate gossip."

"Prudence dear," Millie said. "I on the other hand love gossip. Most of us do. It's like salt and pepper on your food, if you know what I mean. Most of us here, a bunch of old women, widows generally, like me, it gives us a little excitement, so what's the harm?"

"The harm! The poor man is dead."

I tried to steer the conversation into another area. "Mrs. Whetstone tells me you saw Morris's sister, Anna, here, in the building, the day Morris died."

"I suppose. I did see her, in the elevator. I got in the elevator, I'm one floor below them. And she was in the elevator already."

"Coming from Morris's apartment?"

"Presumably."

"And did you notice anything, uh, special or different?"

"Well, she was carrying a big purse, and she was fumbling with it, rummaging around. And, frankly, although I ordinarily wouldn't take any notice, I would just say hello, and that's all . . . but she had a funny look on her face. I mind my own business. I don't pay attention, not usually. Still: in hindsight, it's clear to me what she was doing."

"And what was what?"

"I'd rather not say. It's pure conjecture."

"Ms. Goldfinch: please."

"Alright, I'll tell you. But I don't want this repeated. And it's sheer guesswork. I think she was hiding a gun. I didn't actually *see* the gun, and at the time I had no idea. . . . But now that I've talked to Millicent, now that all this has happened, I have the feeling: that's what it was. She had a gun in her purse. And it wasn't the first time."

"What do you mean by that?"

"I saw her once. In the lobby. And she dropped her purse, and everything spilled out. I distinctly saw what I think was a gun. I am not positive that's what I saw, and what would I know about guns? Still, we see pictures of guns. A gun is a gun. It was a gun."

All this of course made me curious. The rest of the visit passed innocuously. Millicent chattered on, in a harmless way, about weather, the stock market, her daughter, and the way the building was run. It was pleasant enough. Prudence said very little.

I had another piece of apricot tart. Millicent offered to give me the rest of it. "I'll just eat it all up myself, and I'm supposed to be on a diet," she said. "And Abby doesn't each such things. Do take it home, Frank."

But I declined. Reluctantly.

On the way home, as I was driving, I couldn't help thinking about what Millicent had told me; and what Prudence more or less corroborated. But how could I follow up? I had no reason to ask Anna the questions I wanted to ask. I did see her, in my office a few days later—she was, after all, one of the heirs; she had questions about the estate—mostly about the money (which she was so eager to get her hands on). I tried subtly to get her to talk about the day that Morris died. "You were the last person to see him alive," I said to her. "I mean, except for, uh, whoever. . . ."

She ignored my embarrassment. "Oh, yes. If only I had stayed around. I told that to Felicity, and she said, Anna dear, don't be foolish, maybe you would have been killed too. I told her, family is everything, what's life without family; and Morris, he was my dear brother. My only brother, since poor Charlie died. And we hadn't been getting along, as you know. I should have hugged him, I should have put my arms around him; if I had known this was the last time I would ever see him, oh dear, what I would have done. Life can be so cruel sometimes."

"Did he seem . . . well, different?" I asked. "As if something was on his mind?"

"I don't know. Maybe. He did seem . . . reserved. Distant. I said at one point, Morris dear, I don't think you're listening to a word I'm saying. But that only annoyed him, the poor man. Something was on his mind. I think I know what it was."

"Oh? What was it?"

"I can't tell you. It's too private. One thing though: I had the impression somebody was listening in; some nosy person, maybe in the apartment, maybe in the hall way. When I got in the elevator, I thought I heard a door banging. I thought, maybe it's that terrible neighbor, Millicent Whetstone. She and Morris never got along. Never ever."

She changed the subject then, somewhat abruptly, and began asking more questions about the estate. Mostly about when the money would be distributed, and what kind of taxes there were, and would it eat up the estate, she read something about that, the costs, how high they were. She also talked about family, how much family meant to her, and how family was everything, if you don't have family, you have nothing, with all your money, and how her cousin's daughter, Carrie-Anne, had married this billionaire, and how he left her, with two small children and on and on. Of course, she didn't fool me for a minute. She had money on her mind. The thought of inheriting money from Morris evoked visions of sugar plums dancing in her head. And she couldn't understand, or didn't want to understand, why I couldn't simply write out a check for a small fortune and hand it to her, right then and there.

"I don't know why Morris told us that terrible lie," she said. "In the end, he showed us how he really felt, how after all he loved his family. Morris, Morris, I miss him so much. If only he had been able to express himself, men are like that, they can't face emotion, Morris was all locked up, on the outside, but inside, he must have really felt a bond, to his family. After all, when Mother died, who else did he have?"

I was skeptical, to tell the truth, how much Morris really treasured his family—and Anna in particular. But I too was puzzled, of course, at his rather odd behavior. If there was an explanation, it eluded me. And the family as well.

10

As I said, Felicity was a pleasure to work with. She was intelligent and flexible. Under the new will, she was sole executor; I was the lawyer for the estate, but she was formally the one who had to make the decisions. That could have been a problem; but in practice, everything went smoothly. I really liked Felicity.

As for the rest of the family: well, Julia I hardly knew. Anna was annoying, but she was also ineffectual. Felicity knew how to handle her. Then there was Sebastian. In many ways, he was the most interesting of the lot. The baby of the family, probably pampered . . . Aunt Anna's favorite, even though they were so unlike.

Sebastian loved to talk. And talk and talk. I had the impression that somehow, Mother Nature forgot to lock the gates and doors that guard the tongues for most of us. Anything that came into his head went right out his mouth. But what you heard was free, frank, open, completely without malice. All this gave him a certain charm. He had in fact plenty of charm. Besides, he was slim and good-looking, with dirty blond hair, and a dimpled chin; he must have been very attractive to the girls, as indeed he was, according to his own testimony. He was, also, the sort of young man that appealed to older women as well; he struck them less as a stud than as a puppy dog, as a boy who badly needed a mother, and wanted a mother. His own mother had died when he was just a baby. Aunt Anna more or less replaced her.

Sebastian liked money just as much as the rest of the family. Maybe all of us love money. He too was eager to get his hands on at least some piece of the inheritance. He was sitting in my office, and we were discussing the estate. But it was all but impossible to stay on the subject—he kept bringing up other things, like, why did I go to law school? Didn't I find it awfully boring? And what did I think of his sister, Felicity? And, most of all, what did I think of Morris Gross?

"My uncle. The rich uncle. I mean, if he wasn't the most boring man in the world, who is? I suppose there are lots of boring people. I don't want to meet them," he said. "No thank you. I mean, with Morris, you have to wonder, was he actually human? Maybe he was an advanced robot, like you see in the movies. Or, maybe all those years with my grandma did him in. I have to say, I think at the end he had a screw loose. I honestly and totally think so."

I asked him why he had that impression.

"Well, it's kind of a secret. But I know you're not going to tell anybody. Lawyers aren't supposed to. Anyway, it was like this: Uncle Morris had this massive heart attack. Major. And, well, Aunt Anna, she was after me, when he got out of intensive care, she said, Sebastian, you have to visit your uncle. I've been to see him, poor man, and Julia's been, and Felicity went the other day. You have to go. I mean, I didn't care if he lived or died, but I decided to humor Aunt Anna, she's been so good to us, I know she's sort of a hypocrite, but she's got a good heart anyway; so I went to the hospital, you know, Stanford Hospital, I tell you, parking is an absolute nightmare, but anyway, there was Morris, in this room; I hate hospitals, I hate the way they smell, but there I was. And I brought him some flowers and a box of candy. I mean, I couldn't stand the old goat, but he's got all this money, after all, so I came into the room, he was lying there, half asleep, and I said, hi there Uncle Morris. He gave me a look. I said, I brought you these flowers, and a box of chocolates, Belgian chocolates. Of course, he didn't say thank you, that wasn't Uncle Morris, the old creep, instead he said to me, 'you do nothing but waste money. Look at those flowers, they'll only die in a day or two. And how much did you spend on that candy?' That was Morris. A real sweetheart. So I said, well, to be honest, Uncle Morris, I picked the flowers out of a garden, near the place where I live, they were growing there; and some-body gave me the box of chocolates for my birthday. I didn't want to eat them, so I brought them to you. A big lie, but what the hell.

"Anyway, he said, well, then that's OK. Then came this re-ally strange thing. He grabbed my hand, and he said, Sebastian, do you believe in God? And I figured yes was the right answer. I thought, is this guy getting religion or what? He had this heart attack, and now he's getting religious? He said, do you believe in heaven, Sebastian? So I rolled my eyes and I said, oh, I don't know, maybe, I couldn't bring myself to say yes, I mean, the whole idea is ridiculous, where would they all fit, all those dead people. And then he starts telling me this absolutely loony-tunes story, that he died and he went to heaven, and I thought, whoa, where is this coming from? The old man is bonkers. But I made a solemn face, as if I was hanging on every word, and then came the strangest part, he said he saw my grandma, and she told him that somebody murdered her. I looked at him, was he joking? But Uncle Morris never told a joke in his life. I said, Uncle Morris, who have you told about this? He said, nobody, you're the first. So I said, and I'm the last too. Uncle Morris, I said, I believe every word, you wouldn't fool me; but do me a favor, don't tell anybody, it'll be our little secret. You know how people are, they're skeptics, they'll say you're crazy. He said, well, I have to tell my lawyer. I have no idea why he said that, he meant you, Frank; but I said, OK, tell him; but not a word to anybody else. He said, Anna? And I said: Uncle Morris, she's the last person in the world. So he promised me. I said, we've got a deal, we won't breathe a word of this. And of course, I thought, the old boy is out of his mind."

"And did you keep your word? I mean, did you tell any-body?"

"Not a peep out of me. But I have to ask you something. About Uncle Morris. Would it make a difference if he was basically crazy? I mean, what would that do to the will?"

"It could be a problem; but why are you asking? Is it be-cause of the story he told you?

"I mean, what would you think? I never heard such garbage. He must have been out of his mind. Maybe it was the intensive care thing, God knows what they do to you, pump you full of chemicals. Imagine, he thought he went to heaven. There is no such place, to begin with. I mean, there's six billion people on this earth, I think that's what it is, India and China, they all have babies after babies; and all of these people are going to die, and you're not going to tell me they're all going to be up somewhere in the galaxy playing the harp or whatever. Not to mention the gazillion people who died already. I mean, he was hallucinating. But Uncle Morris had all that money, so I was real diplomatic, I mean I tried to be. I tried to make nice, if you know what I mean. I mean, I can lie like anybody else, but you have to sound convincing. Anyway, back to the original question: does it make a difference, if he had some kind of loose screw, about this heaven business?"

"Probably not," I said. "Listen: for one thing, millions of people believe this sort of thing happens. There was this book, written by a kid, I think he was four years old. Well, of course, he didn't really write it, his father was a minister of some sort; the kid had some sort of appendicitis or something, really, really sick; and he swore he had been to heaven and back, where he saw his great grandfather I think and angels with wings; I didn't read the book. Millions of people bought the book; it was a tremendous best seller; they even made a movie out of it, believe it or not."

Sebastian shrugged his shoulders. "I suppose. People believe anything. Noah's Ark. Or reincarnation: can you imagine coming back as a cockroach? This guy, the Dalai Lama, he came to town last year. Thousands of people go to hear him, and he claims he's the old Dalai Lama in a new body, I mean, what kind of nonsense is that? My girlfriend, Abby, she loves the guy. Says he's so spiritual. Never had sex in his life, I guess that's what makes him so spiritual; no thank you, in my opinion. Anyway, Uncle Morris, he told you this heaven story, didn't he?"

"He did."

"You don't believe it, Frank, do you? Come on, don't tell me you buy that kind of thing."

"Not literally," I said. "But something gave him the idea. Something planted it in his mind."

"Maybe he knew something? About Grandma. I mean, let's face it, she was a spiteful old bitch. She knew we hated her, how could you not? And she had her revenge, she left everything to Morris. Listen: I told you, I don't believe in the rubbish he told me. This isn't the Bible belt. But if there was such a place, I mean, heaven, why on earth would Grandma be there? No way. She'd be in the other place, getting whipped by demons or burnt to a crisp or whatever they do there to people who were awful here on earth."

"I'm surprised she cut out your Aunt Anna," I said. "I can understand leaving most of it to your uncle, but all of it? That seems extreme."

"She irritated Grandma; she was always whining and asking for money. Not that she got any. I told you before: the old lady was a spiteful old bitch. If there is, in fact, life up in heaven, or hell, or wherever, she would be cackling with glee to see how disappointed Anna was. Weeping and wailing over the death of her dear mother, and how much she would miss her—but actually, cursing her under her breath."

"And Aunt Martha?"

"Aunt Martha? Grandma was even angrier at her. She committed an unforgiveable sin: she moved away from here, away from Grandma. Grandma considered that an act of treason. . . . No, the only one who deserved the money, as far as she was concerned, was her boy, Morris. And maybe he did deserve it. No life of his own. Just sort of an errand boy for his mother. Year in and year out, there he was, stuck in that condo with a dried up old fossil; maybe he was a fossil himself. Or turned into one."

I tried to steer Sebastian back to estate matters; I was afraid he would spread the story about Morris's voyage to heaven; I thought the less said about it the better. But Sebastian was irrepressible. He loved being in on a secret—something nobody knew except him (and me). "Maybe somebody did kill the old lady. I mean, she was 94 years old, but we always said, she was too mean to die. Somebody got tired of waiting, you know? What do you think?"

"It doesn't seem likely," I said. "They say she died a natural death. A heart attack, I think. They called an ambulance. I mean Uncle Morris did. And Dr. Mel. He was there. The ambulance came, but it was too late. She was dead. Or maybe she died in the ambulance. I don't remember."

"That's what they say. But how do we know? Suppose she was poisoned?"

"Poisoned? Sebastian, get a grip. You can't really think that."

"What about the toothpaste?" he said. "Felicity told me about the toothpaste. Don't you think it's weird, the disappearing toothpaste?"

"Sebastian, you can't be serious. Toothpaste?"

"I think Grandma might have been poisoned with toothpaste. That story about the toothpaste, the thing Anna told my sister. Listen, maybe that was the old lady's toothpaste, not Morris's. He just kept it around. OK, I know it seems ridiculous; but I love ridiculous things. Death by toothpaste! You know, I don't know whether Grandma had false teeth. I don't think she did, but I don't know. My other grandma, she had false teeth, she kept them in a glass at night; it was disgusting. I never saw that at Grandma Gross's place. So if she didn't, if she had her own teeth, then she must have brushed her teeth, doesn't everybody? I mean, I think she did. Every once in while I forced myself to kiss her, like when it was Christmas, and all of us were there; and I never noticed bad breath. I'm very sensitive to smells. Always have been. I went out with this girl once, I thought she was terrific, I was practically drooling, people told me she liked sex; but it turned out, she didn't bother brushing her teeth. One sniff and that was enough. Dropped her like a hot potato."

"Sebastian," I said, "forget the toothpaste. It's just too far-fetched."

"You think? But then why did the toothpaste disappear? I think this is what happened: he saw Anna at the medicine cabinet, Morris did, and he thought: oh my God, it's still there. It's evidence, I mean, you could test it in a laboratory or something. They'd find the poison. So he got rid of it. Or somebody else did. The guilty person. Anybody who was in or out of the place. Frank, I love this. It's like a TV show, crime lab or something, it could be a movie or whatever."

"Sebastian," I said. "If I were you, as I said, I'd forget the toothpaste. You must have better things to do. I certainly do."

But I knew he wouldn't let go. And neither would I let go. Oh, I'd drop the toothpaste . . . but I was not letting go of the death of Bertha Gross.

11

I drove home early. The traffic was horrendous—it always is—but the air was clean and sweet; you could see the fog bank piled on the hills, moving slowly like a river, from the ocean side of the peninsula. California is simply beautiful. Billions of people live somewhere else, I realize, and most of them are perfectly happy where they are. And that's as it should be. If they all moved to California, where would we be?

At home that evening, Celia told me she planned to have people over for dinner.

"Whatever you want, my love," I said.

"I'm going to ask Adam Finkel," she said. Adam was a frequent guest; I've mentioned him before. He's the math teacher at Celia's school, a born loser if you ask me, nice enough, but painfully shy, and with that horrible skin condition. Celia was fond of him. He had become more or less of a project for Celia. One of her goals in life was to provide Adam with a wife, or at least a relationship. "He's tried, poor thing," she said. "Goes on all these websites. If he showed them a picture, that would be the end of it."

"Maybe he should show them some other picture. Brad Pitt," I said.

"Frank, be serious," she said. Celia had a good excuse this time for making dinner. "It's Adam's birthday," she said. "I want to surprise him. I ordered a delicious pear tart, from the bakery, and I'll make something special, something he likes. He must be so lonely! Frank, dear, I'd like you to buy a card, a birthday card, something nice, you can get one at the drug store, the one near your office. I need some stuff from there anyway, and I'm tied up tomorrow. I'll give you a list. Oh, and by the way, Cynthia's getting married, the phys ed teacher, the one with the big nose; I know you don't want to go to the wedding, but we have to go, it would be awful not to. We have to give her a nice present, too. Anyway, I'd like you to get some sort of wedding card."

I usually do what I'm told. After lunch, I went to the local drug store which, like all drug stores, sells so many different things the drug department almost seems like an afterthought. I took a look at the wedding cards; I had a lot of trouble finding one that I thought was suitable. Some of them were bland, inoffensive, basically nothing at all; others were so drippingly sentimental I couldn't bring myself to buy them. Some were deeply religious, and laid on the sacredness of marriage so thick, you might think he was entering a monastery, and she was taking vows in a convent, instead of a relationship which had been or was about to be deeply sexual. Mostly, the cards were frilly, ugly, and filed with extremely bad poetry:

> Two people fell in love
> And swore to heaven above
> They would be true
> One loving pair instead of two.

I finally found one that had a nice picture of a bouquet, and which simply said congratulations and best wishes on your marriage. The birthday cards were also a problem. Funny thing: weddings, after all, do have something to do with sex, but wedding cards never breathe a word of this. Birthdays have nothing to do with sex (I think), yet some of the cards (for adults) were positively raunchy. Here too I finally found something bland and tasteful, suitable for a lonely man with a skin condition.

After I made my momentous card decisions, I wandered over to the toothpaste section. I wanted to look at the toothpastes meant for people with sensitive teeth. I picked up one: Max's of Montana. It was more expensive than the others, but it had that look that said: I'm natural, I'm environmental, I'm not like the commercial brands. I looked carefully at the fine print. There were other toothpastes too that made similar claims, including one called "Sensident." All of them had a warning: Keep out of the reach of children. And this: If a child swallows more than the amount necessary for brushing the teeth, go immediately to the doctor, or call 911.

This impressed me. I started wondering: can you actually poison somebody with toothpaste? Apparently you can do bad things to a child with the toothpaste; and wouldn't a frail, 94 year old woman be vulnerable as well? I knew this was a really weird idea . . . but I couldn't get it out of my brain. I knew that Celia would heap scorn on the very idea. She would bring me back to reality, perhaps a bit roughly. And yet. . . . When I read those warnings, and remembered what Anna had said about the toothpaste, I felt a kind of excitement, a tingling feeling. Could there really be something to this toothpaste theory?

Felicity and I, of course, had a lot to do with regard to the estate. The next time I phoned her, I brought up a number of boring but necessary questions, about gas and electric bills, cable fees, and the like. And then I asked her abruptly: "Felicity, here's a question. I know it'll sound strange. But did your grandmother have false teeth?"

"Frank, that is, in fact, the strangest question I've heard in years. Why on earth are you asking?"

"Humor me, Felicity."

"Well, she didn't, as a matter of fact. She had amazingly good teeth for a woman her age. A couple of implants, a bridge, and a crown or two, I suppose. She was proud of her teeth. Really, I never looked that closely into her mouth. I know she did have trouble with her gums, she was worried about her gums. Gums are pretty important; if the gums go, you're in trouble. But it was nothing serious. I know she went to the dentist regularly. I drove her once, Morris had a cold or something, she went to a dentist in Menlo Park, I forget his name. Dr. Jefferson, I think it was. That was her dentist that particular day; she changed dentists all the time, I think. Typical."

"I don't suppose you know what kind of toothpaste she used."

"Frank: honest to God, now I know what this is all about. It's that ridiculous business with the missing toothpaste. And no, I have no idea what kind of toothpaste my grandmother used, if she used any toothpaste at all. You and Sebastian, I mean, two of a kind. He's going around asking everybody what kind of toothpaste they brush their teeth with. But what in God's name does this possibly have to do with the estate, or with Morris's death, or anything else? And why my grandmother? The woman is dead, after all. She died at a ripe old age."

Of course, I had nothing intelligent to say; and I was not about to tell her the truth: that her grandmother just possibly might have been murdered with a toothbrush or poisoned toothpaste or the like. I did the best I could. "I was just thinking, Felicity, about the missing toothpaste. I was wondering, if it was Morris's toothpaste, or whether it was left over from your grandmother. That's why I asked if she had false teeth."

"You think Morris kept Grandma's toothpaste, as a kind of memento? I mean, Frank, sometimes I wonder about you. Really. I'm sure you're a terrific lawyer and all that, but you get the strangest ideas. I'm sure this toothpaste has nothing to do with anything at all. Just forget it. And don't let Sebastian fill your head with crazy ideas. He has an abundance of those."

The dinner with Adam Finkel went as well as could be expected. The man was terminally shy. Celia had planned to have someone over, a neighbor's daughter, who was the right age, unmarried, and suitably unattractive. "She might be desperate enough to go for him. After all, he's intelligent, he's sweet, and he has a job." But this plan fell through at the last minute. The neighbor's daughter had the flu. Celia was disappointed. Still, she would never give up on Adam. "He'll make somebody a wonderful husband. I know he's got that skin thing. But you see fat people, ugly people, and they're married. I'll find somebody for Adam. I will."

After dinner, when we were drinking coffee and Celia was tempting Adam with a second slice of the pear tart, the doorbell rang. In suburbia, the doorbell never rings unexpectedly, unless it's Jehovah's Witnesses, or Greenpeace with a petition about saving whales, or somebody begging you to work up an interest in a local sewer bond issue.

Celia said, "Who on earth could that be?"

It was, in fact, Sebastian. "You don't mind?" he said. "I'm dying to talk to you, Frank. I'm all excited. I hope I didn't interrupt your dinner."

"No, not at all, Sebastian. We were having dessert and coffee."

"Yum, that looks good," he said, eying the fruit tart. I gave him a slice, and introduced him to Celia and to Adam Finkel, who left rather quickly after that. I think Celia was mildly annoyed, especially because Adam was shy, and she felt that Sebastian, who was anything but shy, had driven Adam away. Sebastian began talking non-stop, about an enormous range of topics, including his family, and the mystery of who murdered his uncle. "I know Frank is working on this," he said.

That was of course the wrong thing to say. Celia bristled. I tried to change the subject, after denying that I was doing anything of the sort.

Celia disappeared into the kitchen to do the dishes—usually my job—and Sebastian sat down in the living room, crossed his legs, and began talking again. "Who was that guy?" he asked. I told him. "Wow, if I looked like that, I'd kill myself. Couldn't he have some sort of operation? What girl would ever look at him twice? I mean, couldn't he wear a mask or something? Like the Phantom of the Opera. Oh well. That's not what I wanted to talk to you about. I'm worried about the will. You know, Morris's will. Now that I think I'm going to get some money, I was reading up about wills and that sort of thing, there's all kinds of websites. You know, when I thought Uncle Morris was going to leave us nothing, not a cent, I thought, wow, I've got to do something. I had this plan, I'd bring a lawsuit, try to break the will."

"Not easy to do, Sebastian."

"Even if he was a total nut-case? Suppose people heard about this trip to heaven. I mean, that was seriously whacked. Maybe his mind was starting to go."

I said, "Sebastian, you know, it's really, really hard to overturn a will. The executor, whoever that would be, he could bring in stock brokers, neighbors, lots of people, and they'd testify that Morris was perfectly competent. I know, that heaven business seems ... strange. But as I told you, millions of people believe that sort of thing. Listen: if a client of mine told me about crazy ideas they had, UFO's, whatever, aliens from outer space, I don't contradict them. And I don't consider them crazy, necessarily. Listen: we all have a quirk or two."

"And anyway," I added, "in the event, it's not in your interest. You're going to get one-ninth of the estate, and that amounts to a lot of money, Sebastian. A lot of money."

"It's a shock," he said. "Boy, I can hardly wait. I have all sorts of plans, Frank. When can I get my hands on that money?"

"Well, hardly right away, Sebastian. You've got to be patient."

"Patience isn't me. You know, I want to try things. Spread my wings, you know? Break out of the mold. I hated college. Booooring. I started law school; that was worse. I dropped out. I'm a free spirit, Frank. I need to experiment, it's my nature. Like: sex. I want to try things. I've had a lot of sex, but, you know, it's like eating, you have a big meal, then you're hungry again. And you don't want the same old thing, if you had a steak, next time you want chicken or whatever. Like: you know, I never made it with a guy, but I'd like to try it some time. Maybe with a lifeguard. I told this to my girlfriend, well, the one I had then, and she just laughed at me. I said, I'm serious. So she said, OK, then, let's do a three-some. It's not going to happen, though. Not with her, anyway. She's history. She was half-Chinese, and I used to say, which half? She had a real sex thing. Wanted to try all the positions in the Kama Sutra or whatever. Some of them, you could get a hernia. But you don't want to hear about my sex life, do you? I didn't think so."

Sebastian's sex life, which, according to him, was quite active, in fact seemed more interesting than what most of my clients talked about. But it was getting late—I was wondering when he would go home, so I could go to bed. There was no stopping him, though.

"Actually, my sex life might possibly be relevant. I mean, I'm a suspect, no? Everybody in the family is a suspect. They say you're secretly investigating things. Cool! You know, Frank, like I told you, nobody liked Uncle Morris, I mean, how could you? He was a real creep. Anyway, back to my sex life. I was visiting Uncle Morris, actually, I wanted to ask him for money. I know, that's not my sex life, but you'll see the connection. As I said, I asked him for money. He said no, of course. But his building, it has a fitness center, and I peeked in—not that Uncle Morris ever set foot in the place, his only exercise his entire life was carrying shopping bags for Grandma, maybe kissing her butt, if that amounts to exercise, but anyway, I looked in, and there's this girl on the treadmill, and I said, oh, hello, do you live in this building; and it turned out, no, she didn't but her mother did, her name was Millicent Whetstone. The mother's name, I mean. This girl was Abby Whetstone. She said, does your family live in this building. No, I said, I've got an uncle who lives here. Morris Gross. She said, oh my God, not Morris Gross. So I said, yes, Morris Gross, what of it? She said, Mother hates him. He's always complaining about noise, Mother's hard of hearing, but she refuses to get a hearing aid, she turns up the TV very loud, and her apartment is next door to his. That's your uncle? Anyway, I said, you can say anything you like about him, he's a real jerk. She was sweating and all that; she looked very sexy, she had that look, you know, her face was all shiny with the sweat, and, well, we started talking, and I said, hey, let's go somewhere, get something to eat, and one thing led to another."

I wanted to hear more about the one thing which led to another, and especially about the thing the one thing led to, but Sebastian suddenly shifted gears again. "She's a terrific person, Abby. I took to her right away. She's vegan. Actually, she's more than that. She won't eat carrots, can you believe it? I said, why not? She says, you kill the plant. When you pull it up, you kill it. They're living things, she says. Same for potatoes. Crazy. I told her I get a thrill out of killing potatoes and carrots; but on this subject, she has no sense of humor whatsoever. I mean, does a carrot suffer? She said, killing is killing."

I tried to imagine life without carrots and potatoes. I do like potatoes, especially french fries. "My God," I said, "what does she eat? I mean, we have to eat something."

"Well, nuts, apples, you don't kill the tree; maybe she eats lettuce and that sort of thing. I guess she doesn't mind killing a head of lettuce; it's a very restricted diet, but hey, it's her body. She says it leaches all the poison out of the system. I said, I guess I enjoy the poison. Fortunately, it didn't leach all the sex drive out of her. Maybe if you live like that, you've got to have sex. She uses birth control, so I guess she doesn't mind killing zillions of sperm cells, but then, they're not potatoes, are they? I tried to be a vegetarian once, somebody told me it was great, you'd have the most terrific bowel movements. Lasted a week. It just wasn't me, and the bowel movements were nothing special. Well, I'm off gluten now, that's my current thing. I mean, I really don't have the slightest idea what gluten is, but I like the idea, you know 'gluten free' this and 'gluten free' that. I'm eating potatoes, meat, all I want. But no gluten. At least not today. Who knows what I'll do tomorrow?"

I was getting sleepy, but Sebastian just went on and on. I wanted him to go; but still, I could see why people liked him. The flow of talk—you wondered what was coming next. But it wasn't dull. Anyway, I crossed him off the list of suspects. I couldn't imagine him with the sort of rage, or cunning, that it would take to kill Morris Gross. Maybe that was a mistake. People can fool you.

"This murder excites me, Frank," he said. "I mean, who would kill Uncle Morris? True, nobody liked him, except Grandma, and she was a rotten, dried-up prune if there ever was one. . . . But I've got a theory. . . . You know, my girlfriend Abby. Maybe she killed Uncle Morris."

"Your girlfriend?"

"Current girlfriend. You know, they don't last long with me. I guess I'm always looking for something new. That's the way I am. I know it isn't good. But, hey! Anyway, Abby, she's an actual suspect. She's a real new-age person, you know the type, she says, money is a trap, people with money are prisoners; I said, OK, Abby, make me a prisoner, I'd love it. Anyway, she's been like that for years. She told me she wanted to live in a commune, one time she sort of tried it, she dropped out of school, with a boyfriend, another weirdo like her, and they wanted to live in the woods and grow pot, make their own clothes, who knows, gather berries or whatever, grow vegetables, but no carrots thank you, no TV, smoke dope, and so on. They moved in with a bunch of like-minded weirdos, boys and girls. They lived in some sort of shack or hut, God knows what. It lasted a year. Half of the girls got pregnant, who knows who the fathers were. Abby, she didn't get pregnant. I think she still had too much sense. Or maybe she tried to be a born-again virgin or something. Whatever. It didn't last. She got tired of the whole business. Can't say I blame her. I mean, what do you do all day? I mean, nature, it's great, I love to hike in the woods, but to live there? Me, I'd rather be dead."

I nodded my head. I kept thinking: how long was he going to stay?

"Abby's folks were divorced," he said. "The father, he was supposed to be really awful. He's dead now. When Abby was in Mendocino, on this commune, her dad had a fit. He was actually a Republican. She has two brothers, too. They stuck with their father, and Abby doesn't see them. Just as well. They went to business school, a fate worse than death. Her mother, she was the only one that was halfway decent; I love Millicent. She's a character, she loves to laugh, and she gets along with Abby. Well, mostly. Abby—actually, this piece of land, the one with the shack on it, in Mendocino, it belonged to her. She had money from some dead relative, a grandmother I think, or maybe her father; that's how she came to buy the land. Mendocino is full of rich people, but the crazy kind. And when she got tired of this nature business, she kicked the others out and sold the land. Made quite a bit of money, by the way. Then she went with some other guy, they moved to Iowa, big mistake. This guy, his name was Harold, and they were making furniture and selling it on the web. Ugliest stuff I ever saw, a chair shaped like a penis, if you can imagine such a thing. She told me the whole story. God knows where she picked him up, he doesn't look like Iowa to me, but what do I know about Iowa? Never been there.

Cornfields, that's my image of Iowa. She dumped this guy, and moved back here. Got a job, an apartment. She's a lot more normal. Well, sort of."

"She doesn't live in the building, does she?"

"No, of course not. It's like an old people's home; nobody young lives there, I swear. And the prices are outrageous. Sometimes she stays with her mother, though. They get along, so long as Abby doesn't spend too much time and gets out before they get on each other's nerves. She's got a place in San Jose. Or she stays with me. She's the restless type. But she's OK. For now anyway. Except, she likes to go barefoot. I find that disgusting. I have a thing about dirty feet. And God knows what you might be stepping into—nails, glass, dogshit, whatever."

Where was this going?

"OK, you're wondering," Sebastian said, "why is this guy, this Sebastian, why is he telling me all this stuff? Felicity says, I talk too much. Can't help it. She's always saying, Sebastian, get to the point. OK, here's the point. Abby has that money, from when she sold the land. She wants to start a restaurant, vegan, in fact, super-vegan, no carrots and potatoes. I told her, nobody would eat in such a restaurant, but I could be wrong; there are so many food crazies here, you wouldn't believe it. She's got some of the money, she's got some guy lined up, he's going to be the chef, if she ever gets this thing off the ground. Right now, this chef works for some fancy restaurant in Palo Alto, but he fights with the owner all the time, so he's looking for something different. But the rents around here, they're unbelievable, nobody can afford anything, so she needs more money, cash, she needs some kind of angel."

"Are you thinking of your own money? The money from the estate?"

"God no, I'm not *that* crazy. I might as well flush the money down the toilet. Really. No, not me. She said to me, Sebastian, you've got a rich uncle. Filthy rich. Maybe he'd like to invest in me, you know, venture capital. I said, he won't give you a penny. She said, how do you know? I can be very persuasive. I said, hey, Abby, you can try. I mean, Uncle Morris won't give money to his relatives, so he certainly won't give money to a total stranger. Especially a girl with tattoos on her ankle. And especially Abby, when he and her mother are like cats and dogs. I said, Abby, what are you going to do, how are you going to talk him into it? You going to offer your body to the old goat? And she said, well, he might try it and like it; but I have a different idea."

"A different idea? Like what?"

"I honestly don't know. But this idea popped into my head. Maybe she killed him. It could have been robbery or something like that. I mean, Abby is capable of anything. I really think so. Maybe that's what I like about her. I get all tingly, thinking about her. Just the thought of her, and I can get, well, an erection. I mean, you can't predict what she's going to say, or do, or think. She kept telling me, I think maybe I could get something out of your uncle. I said, hey, Abby, how? She said something funny. She said: I know something. I've got some information and it might be worth money to your uncle, you know? I said, go right ahead Abby, you say you've got information, and it's worth money, I have to tell you, nothing is worth money to Uncle Morris, except more money, as far as I know, but hey, maybe you should go ahead and try."

"But she didn't tell you what happened?"

"I asked her, but she wouldn't tell me. None of your business, you know, that sort of thing. I said, hey, it *is* my business, he's my rich uncle. So I'm thinking: maybe she murdered him. For the money. Not that she got any money out of the guy, that's impossible; even if she was trying to blackmail him. How could she blackmail him, by the way? How could you blackmail a guy, who never goes out of the house, except maybe to the dentist and that sort of thing. But maybe she broke in, she thought there was great stuff there, and uncle Morris caught her in the act, I mean, who knows?"

"What would she steal? I thought there was nothing much in the house to steal."

"Not that I know of. I mean, sure, a gigantic TV set, furniture, that sort of thing, but nothing else. Uncle Morris wasn't the type to keep cash under the mattress, and the pictures on the wall weren't worth two cents, if you ask my opinion. But who knows? She might have been on to something. Anyway, that's my latest theory."

"I hope you didn't tell Abby about your theory. Or the police, for that matter."

"Frank, I'm telling you, not the police. It's more fun this way. Anyway, about the police, look, I'm a suspect, right? I better stay away from them. And Abby, if I told her, she'd cut my balls off, I swear. No, not a word."

"Then why are you telling me, Sebastian?"

"So you can investigate. . . . I know that's what you're doing. Talk to Abby, check it out. You know, be clever, ask little questions, tricky ones, lawyers know how to do that; and maybe, who knows, something will slip out. . . . People say, you're really clever about these things. I wouldn't have thought so, you don't seem like a great detective, meaning no offense. But everybody's talking."

You know I hate that idea. Frank May the Sherlock Holmes of San Mateo. But once an idea like this gets born, there seems to be no way on earth to get rid of it. I protested as much as I could; but I'm sure Sebastian paid no attention.

"I know you have to say that," he said.

"I don't have to say that. I'm saying it because it's so."

"OK, have it your way," he said. "Promise at least that you'll meet Abby, talk to her. I'll set up a lunch."

I could hardly say no. At that point, Celia came back into the room, obviously irritated that Sebastian was still there; she announced that she was going to bed, it was late, she had to get up in the morning, and it was a pleasure meeting Sebastian. Even Sebastian, who seemed tone-deaf in some ways, got the hint. He left shortly later.

12

As soon as Sebastian left, Celia asked, "Who *was* that?"—although I had told her before. Celia, unlike the rest of the world, seemed to be impervious to his charms. "And why on earth did he come here? At night. He could see you at your office."

I had no real defense for Sebastian. Celia was right, as usual. Clients *can* be demanding; they are men and women and businesses with problems, big and small; and their problems always loom larger in *their* lives than they do in mine. So they sometimes telephone at night. But dropping in: no, that was almost a first.

And Sebastian wasn't even a client. Or not exactly a client. The estate was my client; and Sebastian was one of the beneficiaries, so in a way I had to treat him as a client. And clients get kid glove treatment.

They're the source of my income. I need them for the mortgage, for feeding the family, for vacations, for money in the bank. Celia earns money, but most of it goes into a college fund for our daughters. Colleges have become fearfully expensive.

I don't have time, or inclination, to play the role of the great detective, even if I had even the slightest glimmer of talent. The great detectives have a dangerous job, judging from the mysteries I read. They seem to find themselves in dark alleys, where some desperate character clubs them over the head. They also, it seems, climb into bed with beautiful, sexy women who are also suspects. Sherlock Holmes on the other hand was apparently sexless; but more recent detectives, in novels at any rate, are incredible studs. If I went in for that, it would be Celia, not a desperado, who would club me on the head. And I would deserve it.

It was far more important to do a good job with the estate of Morris Gross, than to find out who killed him. This estate was one of the best I had ever had. Very few of my clients were as rich as Morris Gross. I could sit, daydreaming, about all the things I could buy with the fee. A trip to Italy was high on my list. Celia would like that, of course; but she was also thinking of the Sub Zero refrigerator, the kitchen, and remodeling the back bathroom. "The tile is cracked," she told me. I could live with cracked tile, but Celia had standards.

To be honest, I had no hope of figuring out who killed Morris Gross. For all I knew, the police were on the verge of making an arrest. OK: I admit it: I was intrigued. It was, after all, a strange affair. And I was getting to know the cast of characters—the likely suspects—which made it even more intriguing.

And then there was the death of Bertha Gross. Now *that* was tantalizing. Did somebody really get rid of the old lady? Why did Morris Gross think so? And if somebody did the bloody deed, how and why was it done?

I met periodically with Felicity, who was after all the executor. The more I saw of her, the more I liked her. She was completely unlike Sebastian. Felicity was divorced. Her ex-husband had done something in the computer business. "The less said about him, the better," she said. "He's history." She did tell me that she got fed up because "he was never home. He spent all his time with these two other guys, Hal and Windy. Especially Hal. They were inseparable."

"Were they, uh, lovers?"

"I wish. No. Business partners. They were all consumed with business, making money, getting rich in Silicon Valley. They wanted to be billionaires. After a while, I just couldn't stand it and I got a divorce. I don't think he even noticed."

What was galling was that Merton, the ex-husband, *did* eventually make real money. He started some computer thing with Hal and Windy; and then sold it to Google for some colossal amount. Now Merton was married again, to an Indian woman in a sari. "I wish her good luck," Felicity told me. "She's pregnant, too."

"Well, at least they have sex," I said to Felicity.

"You think? I'll bet it's artificial insemination," she said. "Merton can't take time out for that other kind of thing."

It was a lot of work, managing an estate as large as the estate of Morris Gross. But Felicity and I were a good team. And the accountant too was a huge help; the financial end of the estate was in excellent shape.

I felt comfortable enough with Felicity, after a while, to ask sly questions about her late grandmother—about Bertha's life and (especially) her death. We were having lunch together, which we did periodically. Felicity, like every other woman I know, was on a diet; but also like every other woman I know, she strayed off course once in a while. She had a real love for sushi. We met in a nice little Japanese restaurant, near 3rd Street in San Mateo.

"I adore sushi," she said. "I draw the line at sea urchin, though."

I draw the same sort of line; but we had fun with other kinds of sushi. "Tell me about your grandmother," I said, in between fatty tuna and yellow tail.

"Oh dear," she said. "Bertha Gross. You know, we really didn't like her. None of us. Well, there was Morris, but that's different. How could we like her? All my friends had these sweet old grandmas who pampered them. We could have used one of those. Oh, my other grandmother: she was OK, but she was far away. We were a really screwed up family; my father, Charlie, he was sweet to us, but frankly, he was a real loser. My mother was dead, Sebastian was just a baby when she died. Father married this horrible creature, Jasmine. Of course, Grandma was absolutely savage on this subject; but that's water under the bridge."

"How often did you visit your grandmother?"

"Well, we used to go to the condo once in a while. When we were summoned. Christmas, that sort of thing. The whole family. She insisted on it; and we all went. I think, actually, it was because she was so rich. Why else would anybody cater to her? It was sheer torture. She spent half her time complaining about everything, the food, the weather, politics, her family, how we all neglected her, and why was this one wearing these terrible clothes, and why didn't Sebastian get a haircut, and wasn't Julia's dress too short, it was disgraceful, blah blah; and the rest of the time she was giving us orders, what she wanted us to do, how to behave, and so on, and barking out commands, especially to Morris, of course; her live-in slave. She ordered him around as if he was some kind of servant. All he would say is yes Mother, sure Mother, and so on. Well, he had the last laugh I suppose. He got the money. Fat lot of good it did him, Frank. And now he's dead."

"When is the last time you saw your grandma?"

"Let me see. Well, first of all, there was this family gathering, it was a few days before she died. In fact, we were all there, Aunt Anna, me, Sebastian, Julia; even Aunt Martha; she was visiting, at the time. Grandma was just horrible to her, reduced her to tears. And of course Uncle Morris was there."

"Was there some special occasion?"

"I think it was her birthday. She used to have everybody over, on her birthday. That neighbor, Millicent, she brought in some sort of dish she cooked, some lasagna-like substance, it was absolutely vile, to be honest. A nice woman. Cheerful. I think Grandma sort of liked her, strange as it seems. You know, Morris and Millicent quarreled terribly after Grandma died. To be more accurate, Morris quarreled with her; I don't know why. He would have nothing to do with her. But this was before all that happened. Anyway, Millicent was there. You know that Sebastian is having a thing with Millicent's daughter these days. But at that time, it was somebody else. I can't keep up with him, really. They don't last long, his girlfriends. Maybe this one will. Abby. She might be the right one for Sebastian, by the way. Just as flaky as he is."

"And that was the last time you saw your grandmother?"

"Well, no. Not really. I came, well, it was a few days before she died. I was in downtown Palo Alto, and I thought I'd visit. No particular reason. I guess—Frank, I'm only human, the woman was filthy rich, she was my grandmother, and she was

94 years old. She seemed indestructible, but I thought, you can't tell at that age, she could go at any minute. So, yes, I was trying, hard as it was, to get on her good side. Not that I made much of an impression. She was as tough as nails."

"So, just a visit," I said.

"Yes, but . . . Aunt Anna was there, to my surprise. She and Grandma were sitting in the living room, and they looked . . . strange. Like they had been quarreling. I didn't see Morris. I think he must have been in another room. You could cut the atmosphere with a knife, it was so . . . hostile, I think. Or something else. I couldn't tell. But Grandma was more than usually rude. She said, what do you want, Felicity? We're busy. I said, oh, I'm sorry to butt in then, I was just wondering, I'm going shopping, at the grocery, did you need anything."

"And she said?"

"She said there was nothing she needed. In a nasty tone of voice. She said Morris takes care of that. She clearly wanted me to go. On the way out, I heard her saying to Anna, in a loud voice, something like, 'I won't have it. I won't have that kind of scandal in my family. I won't put up with it.' I stood there, with the door half open . . . I wanted to hear the rest. But just then Millicent came out of her apartment, and gave me a bright hello, and I couldn't just keep on standing there, so I closed the door and went home."

"And you never found out what this was all about?"

"Never. I wanted to ask Aunt Anna, what was going on? Was Grandma mad at you? But—well, frankly, I love Aunt Anna, I owe so much to her, but she's not exactly the most honest, truthful person in the world. Let me give you an example. I was away at college, and I came home for Christmas, and I said to Aunt Anna, how's everybody, how's Grandma Gross, and she said, she's fine . . . and then I asked her about the other grandma, my mother's mother, a dear sweet woman, Grandma Tilden, the one in Kansas City, and Anna said, oh, darling, I heard she died last month; I didn't want to tell you, you had your college work, your exams, and all that, I didn't want you to get upset. I didn't say anything, but I thought what she did was completely wrong, appalling in fact. I was angry for a while.

Hurt. But then I stopped. Aunt Anna means well. I have to be grateful to her."

We had finished eating by then, and I paid the bill, and walked Felicity to her car. As I went back to my office, I kept thinking: what *were* they quarreling about, Anna and her mother? If only Felicity had heard more of the conversation. In any event, I had to consider Anna one of the prime suspects. It was hard to imagine her as a killer. But then who else?

13

The lunch with Sebastian and Abby was uneventful, in every way. She was a pretty young woman, with long braided hair, all sorts of necklaces, rings, and bracelets, of every conceivable color and material, and earrings that seemed a foot long to me. She wore a skirt down to her ankles, in what I imagine to be peasant style, and sandals. At least she wasn't barefoot this time.

Sebastian had made a reservation in an "Asian fusion" restaurant, featuring seafood, among other things. He and Abby came in together, about fifteen minutes late.

Abby didn't make much of an impression on me. During the lunch, she said very little—whether because that was her personality, or because she had no particular urge to talk to a lawyer like me. No matter: Sebastian did enough talking for the three of us.

And she hardly touched any food. "I told you, Abby is funny about food," Sebastian said. "Sometimes I wonder how she stays alive."

"I eat very well," she said. "Healthy food. Eating meat is barbaric. Fish too. Or chicken and other dead birds. We have no right to make these creatures suffer. Do you know how we treat chickens, it's disgraceful, the way we keep them penned up. They have absolutely no life."

"Have an oyster," Sebastian said. "Oysters have no brains. There's no such thing as a suffering oyster."

"It's a living creature," she said. In the end, all she ate was a salad, and an apple that she took out of a gigantic, wicker purse.

I never got to ask her any of the questions I wanted to ask. Which was just as well. I had no idea how to confront her.

She left before Sebastian. He grinned and said, "Isn't she something?"

I had to admit she was something. Everybody is something. He followed me to my office, in fact, he followed me right into my office, and sat down in a chair across from my desk, as if he meant to stay for a while, which I dreaded. He asked whether I had some time to talk. I think he meant some time for *him* to talk, and me to listen. I said, "Well, a little bit, Sebastian. But don't overdo it."

He asked me: "What have you found out? I mean, you've been investigating. How's it coming?"

"Sebastian, I'm not investigating."

"I am, though. I'm studying the whole situation, it's got me more excited than anything since the first time I had sex in a public park. What did you think of Abby? Do you think she might have done it? I don't rule her out. I saw this movie once, not that it's relevant, and this guy, he has sex with this really dangerous woman, and at the end, they have sex again, and when it's over they kill each other. Not that I want to die, but the thought, maybe Abby killed my uncle, it kind of spices things up, if you know what I mean. Anyway, suppose she was at her mother's that night. They could both be in on it. There's no alibi. I mean, they could give each other an alibi, but who's going to believe them?"

"Why would she kill your uncle? Be serious, Sebastian."

"Well, he was trying to get her mother evicted. Called the building owner, was constantly complaining, about the noise. I mean, Uncle Morris was a colossal creep. I told Abby, hey, you've got a motive. She said to me, don't be ridiculous. I said, he was trying to force your mom out of the building, you know, force her to sell. That's not nice. I love your mother. She said, do you now. She doesn't always get along with her mother, as a matter of fact. But maybe she killed Morris, to get him off her mother's back. If they got rid of Millicent, maybe she'd have to move in with Abby. Maybe it's worth killing the guy to prevent that."

"Sebastian, that's ridiculous."

"I know, I know. But somebody did kill him. I like the idea of blaming Abby. I mean, we're getting tired of each other anyway. It would be a neat way to break up with her, her getting arrested, and so on. I'd get on TV. I'd be famous. Interview with the ex-boyfriend. Or boyfriend. Anyway, she did try to blackmail Uncle Morris. I told you that. I know blackmail is a dirty word, but it's true. What she was blackmailing him about, I have no idea. I can't imagine Uncle Morris doing anything worth getting blackmailed about. But who knows."

"Sebastian," I said, "I have work to do. I haven't got time to listen to all this."

"OK, OK. But wait a minute. I keep thinking and thinking. If it isn't Abby, who is it? Maybe it's one of us. The family. Wow. Of course, I know I didn't kill Uncle Morris, unless somebody put me in a trance, or hypnosis or something. I saw a movie once where that happened. This guy, the detective, he's searching for the killer—hot on the trail, and the killer, it's him, but he doesn't know it. He was under hypnosis. OK, that's not the case. Still, who did kill the old geezer? You're going to think this is crazy, but could it be maybe Felicity?"

"Come on, Sebastian," I said. "Your sister? Anyway, I work with her all the time, on the estate. She's not the murdering type."

"You can never tell," he said. "You know, she's a lot older than me. Julia's in the middle. She's pretty much older too. I'm the baby in the family. I think I was an accident, you know? I think my folks thought, two was enough, which it usually is. And then, pop, I came along. I love the idea, the accident idea. You know, I think that's why I'm the way I am, I mean, it's because I wasn't planned. Do you think that's crazy?"

"I don't think it's crazy," I said, "but what difference would it make, if you were planned, unplanned, or what?"

"Oh, maybe nothing. But I used to have these fantasies. My parents ... you have to remember, I didn't really know my mother. . . . She died when I was a baby, all I have are a few photographs, which is nothing much. Felicity remembers her of course. Anyway, I like to think: my folks, they were careful, very careful, careful people, you know, like Uncle Morris and Aunt Anna, and they planned everything, two kids, that's fine, can't afford more children, and so on. They probably used whatever contraceptives people used back then in the dark ages; but then, this is what I think, one night, hey, they like slipped up, or they had a mad passion that they couldn't resist, I mean, anyway, like, wow! And there they were, they were helpless, I mean, sex makes you helpless, when you really get into it, if you know what I mean. And boom! That was me. That was what came out of it. Me. So, I'm different from my sisters. They were planned, I was spontaneous. I think it makes a difference, don't you? From the beginning, the big bang, if you get my point. I'm not like the rest of the litter. Especially Julia. Have you met Julia?"

"Yes . . . I can't say I know her well—but yes, I've met her."

"Don't get me wrong. I love her. She's my sister. But she's colorless, she's invisible. You can see through her, it's like she isn't there. I once said to her, Julia, get a life. Flap your wings. She has the mentality of . . . I don't know what. Maybe a woman who wears glasses, and works in a library and is always shushing people up. Not that she wears glasses. She has contact lenses, you know? I hate contact lenses, people are always losing them; I'd rather squint a little. Anyway, you know what I'm saying. About Julia. No life. I think she's actually a virgin. I asked her once, I said, sister dear, are you a virgin? She was very annoyed with me, but that's nothing new."

I was tempted to ask what Julia's answer was. "I think she actually was a genuine actual virgin," he said. "Four years of college, and nothing to show for it but a bachelor's degree, if you know what I mean. But hey, maybe she's just a late bloomer. Maybe she's not a virgin any more. Or won't be, soon enough. She's madly in love with this guy Johnny. The lawyer's son, you know who I mean, Johnny Mills. She's like a lovesick puppy around him. I don't think he gives a hoot for her; but I'm sure if he wanted her precious virginity, she'd give it to him in a heartbeat."

I reminded Sebastian again that I had work to do. He said, "OK, OK, I'm going. But Julia. . . . Why did I bring her up? As a suspect, Frank. I mean, she seems totally unlikely, but who knows? Maybe she just snapped, you know? She thought she was going to get a lot of money. She was tired of her boring life. She wanted money, it gives you wings, you can fly away. She might be like Lizzie Borden: I mean, who would have thought, Lizzie Borden, a dried up spinster, then she took an axe and bashed in her parents' heads. Disgusting. I mean, an uncle, that's not like killing your parents. And Uncle Morris, I mean, give me a break, maybe somebody did the world a favor, getting rid of him."

Sebastian got up, and tugged at his pants. I could see the tops of his polka-dot underwear. He ran his fingers through his hair. "Mark my words," he said. "This is all about money. Why else would anybody kill Uncle Morris? He was this old creep, sitting on a pile of money, that's the key to the whole business anyway. Frank, if you really want to go into this, remember what I said about Julia. And then there's Felicity. She's the oldest, and she sort of raised us. I mean, yes, Aunt Anna, she gets the credit, but do you know Aunt Anna? I mean, she's hopeless. But Felicity was always there for me. She was like my mother sometimes. I said, Felicity, you're strong. You can do anything."

I practically pushed him out the door. I had a deadline to meet. But I couldn't help thinking about what he said. There was no question, all four of them had a motive, and the motive was money. But I had no time, really, to spend on Morris Gross at the moment. I had clients coming in. So I shoved to one side the Great Detective act, and went to work on more mundane matters.

14

I've been involved before in tangled matters, crimes that somehow swept me into the web, but I was always perfectly able to concentrate on other kinds of work. Of course, with regard to Morris Gross, that wasn't necessarily a different matter; I was, after all, handing the estate, together with Felicity . . . and that meant it was often on my mind, for perfectly good professional reasons.

A day or two after my conversation with Sebastian—if you can call it a conversation, since he did all the talking—I had an urgent meeting with Felicity. Our investment adviser was pressing us to sell a group of bonds, which he considered risky. Montana school bonds, as I recall; or was it something to do with Detroit? Whatever. After we came to a decision, I couldn't resist saying to her, "You know, Felicity, I can't help wondering about that letter. . . . The one that we were supposed to find in the condo, the one that was supposed to tell us that somebody or other wasn't going to get any money. I doubt whether the letter would have any validity, I mean, legally speaking. Still, it might be important. So I'm thinking: who had access to the envelope? Who could have taken it?"

"I just don't know," she said. "I suppose all of us. I mean, the family. We weren't there that much, and God knows Uncle Morris wasn't in the habit of inviting people over; but I suppose we were there at one time or another. And when we were there, I mean, we'd have to go to the bathroom, or into the kitchen, so it's not like Morris was watching us all the time. And, oh yes, it's not just family. Maybe Dr. Percival; I know he saw Morris professionally, Morris had that terrible heart attack, and the doctor, who, after all was a friend of the family, used to check up on him from time to time. It would be easy to take the letter out of the envelope, and put the will back into another envelope and seal it."

"Anybody else? Beside the doctor, and the family?"

"Frank, I have no idea. I just wasn't keeping track. It could have been a salesman. I mean, I don't think so, but I have no idea who was in and out of the house. He had a cleaning service, once every two weeks. Maybe there were other people. Repairmen, or something."

"Neighbors?"

"Well, he hated Millicent. I'm sure she never came by. Prudence Goldfinch? I don't think so. She used to visit Grandma, but after that, I don't imagine she would drop in on Morris. But maybe not. And there was some man on the fourth floor, Ezra something, who *maybe* once in a while visited Uncle Morris. Beyond that, I just don't know.

Morris's behavior had certainly been odd, to say the least. I tried to imagine his thought processes. If he felt that somebody was responsible for his mother's death, he would want to cut that person out of his will (assuming they were in it). He told everybody he was disinheriting the lot, and giving the money to charity, in memory of his mother. Of course that was a big disappointment to them. It was also a lie. I guess—and it's just a guess—that he didn't want to tip his hand. Suppose (just suppose) he wanted to cut out Felicity, but wasn't willing to let on that he suspected her. He told the lie, then wrote out the holograph, giving the money back to the innocent members of the family; and then he wrote a separate letter, to me, which named the name of the guilty person. Let's say it's Felicity's name. The point was, that person was not to get a penny of his money.

In fact, as I had suggested to Felicity, you can't modify a will simply by writing a name on a piece of paper, and putting it in an envelope. I know that, and other lawyers know that, but then we're law-trained members of the California bar. Morris most definitely was not a law-trained member of the bar.

Maybe Morris thought this was a good way to handle this delicate matter. In any event, somebody got wind of his scheme, and simply took the letter and destroyed it. Was this before or after Morris died? Or maybe *during*? By that I mean, while this person, he or she, was getting rid of Morris . . . or right about that time. After all, this person was presumably responsible for Bertha's death; and now was getting rid of Morris. I shuddered involuntarily. It was a chilling thought.

All the more so, if this was somebody I knew; someone I had spoken to, and seen face to face.

15

The last thing I needed was more interaction with Sebastian, but that's what I got. I had had a productive morning. When I drove to work, the morning fog, all chilly and silvery, was receding, and a brilliant sun came out. The traffic was less killing than normal, and the dry, bracing air reminded me for the thousandth time why all of us love California.

At noon, I treated myself to lunch at a local dim sum restaurant, regretting only that I wasn't with other people, so that we could share more dishes. When I came back from lunch, there was Sebastian, waiting outside my office, in the corridor. He was wearing a bright orange T-shirt, with Chinese characters on it. "Sebastian, what's up?" I said.

"Progress report, Frank," he said, sitting himself down in front of my desk, and crossing his legs. I had a feeling in the pit of my stomach that Sebastian was planning a protracted stay. And I was really busy.

Don't get me wrong. I liked Sebastian. I found his eagerness infectious.

"Progress?" I said. "About what?"

"The murder, of course. I've been working on the toothpaste."

"Oh God, not the toothpaste."

"Frank, get real. It's an actual clue, the toothpaste. Think about it. Why would somebody take the toothpaste? Maybe nobody took the toothpaste. Uncle Morris threw it out, and bought a different kind. But why would he do that? I'm excited by the toothpaste, Frank. I've been following up on it, I think it means something. I have no idea what it means, but I'm sure it's a clue. Do you like to read mysteries? They're full of clues. You have to be smart to notice them, they're planted all over the book. I have to admit, I never guess who did it. I don't even try. Sometimes, I just go to the back of the book, and find out who did it, instead of being in suspense all the time. I get these books at a used book store, they don't cost anything, and after I read them, I throw them in the garbage."

"Whoa, Sebastian. . . . You say you've been following up on this? What on earth do you mean?"

"The toothpaste, Frank. I'm really excited. I'm doing re-search. Uncle Morris used a dentist named Ryan Dobbs, I think you know him, a right-wing creep, but I guess he's a good dentist. He's pretty new, so he wasn't Grandma's dentist, I can't find out much about her dentist, she kept changing dentists . . . at one time, she went to some guy named Caleb something, right near your office, actually. But the guy moved out of town, there was some sort of scandal, whatever."

I knew all about this "scandal," an affair (a murder in fact), in which I had gotten quite involved. Caleb had been my dentist too. But it didn't seem relevant to talk about this, so I held my tongue. Sebastian went on: "So this Dobbs guy, he said he didn't know. Kind of nasty about it, too. He said, this is a free country, so far anyway, and we don't force people to use this or that kind of toothpaste—what Mr. Gross used was entirely his own business. This Dobbs was a real nut. Tea Party type. I suppose he thinks Obama wants to take our toothpaste away, along with light bulbs and guns. Anyway, that was a dead end."

"Sorry, Sebastian."

"Hey, Frank, I don't give up so easily, you know? I started asking people in the family, I wanted to find out, who uses that kind of toothpaste. And I got an answer: Julia. I called her up and asked her, Julia, sister dear, what kind of toothpaste do you use? She said, why are you asking? Julia thinks I'm a bit unhinged, and maybe I am. Listen, there's a lot of worse things than being like me. At least *I* think so. So I said, never mind why I'm asking, just tell me. She says, what do you mean? What brand? I said, sure, what brand. And she said, well, it's called

'Sam's Sensitive Teeth,' if you must know. And I thought: wow! Home run. So I asked her, where do you get this, anyway, I don't see it on the shelves at Walgreens. She said, it's on sale in a health food store. Really, Sebastian, she says, what are you driving at? But I made her tell me the whole story. She had some kind of mysterious toothache, this was two years ago, and she went to her dentist, Flansbaum, and he checked and took X-rays, but didn't find anything. I don't like those X-rays. Could make you sterile, you know? I won't let my dentist do it."

"I suppose lots of people use that type of toothpaste," I said. "It's not just on sale in health food stores."

California is full of health nuts. People patronize health-food stores, they pay premium prices, and they buy bee pollen, organic apricots, palmetto leaves and a lot of other products, most of them, in my opinion, completely useless.

"Don't sneer," he said. "Listen: it cured her toothache right away. Of course, I didn't ask her, did you steal Uncle Morris's toothpaste? She'd say no, naturally."

"Sebastian," I said, "far be it from me to criticize your excellent detective work. But what on earth does it have to do with the case? Suppose Julia does use this toothpaste. So what? How does that fit in with what happened to your Uncle Morris? Anyway, if Julia used this toothpaste, then why would she take toothpaste from Uncle Morris's? And why would she keep her toothpaste in his medicine cabinet in the first place?"

"Good point. Still . . . did you ever look at this kind of toothpaste, what it says on the tube? Keep out of the reach of children. If you swallow a bunch of it, call poison control, and that sort of thing. Kind of eye-opening, isn't it? Grandma was poisoned by toothpaste. I'm sure of it."

"Maybe *you* are sure, Sebastian . . . but I'm not." I was ashamed to tell him I had myself looked at these brands of toothpaste in the drug store.

"Won't you be surprised when I crack the case. Maybe I should become a detective. I have to be something. So far, looks like I'm pretty much of a zero. A loser. A nice loser, a loser with sex appeal, but hey, I'm still a loser. Nowadays you have to have some sort of profession. That's what Aunt Anna keeps telling me. Well, I did go to college, Santa Cruz, I got through it some-how. But I'm not suited for anything. I had this law course, I liked the prof, that is, when I went to class, which was once in a while, but the material, I mean, talk about boring! And to think of a lifetime reading that stuff, no thank you. I'm a people person. I don't know how I'm going to make a living. To tell the truth, I'd love to be independently wealthy. I don't want to work at all. Most jobs are too dreary."

"Well, maybe life is dreary, Sebastian. Money doesn't grow on trees. You're luckier than most people—you're actually going to inherit money, which is something that doesn't happen to most people. Anyway, there must be some job you'd like. Look, Sebastian, take my own job. There's some drudge work, yes, but for the most part, Sebastian, I like what I do. I get to talk to people like you, for instance."

"But how many people are like me? Don't answer that, Frank. I'm one of a kind. You know that. I was born to have fun. I see life closing in on me. I spent the last year examining my options, if you know what I mean."

"No, frankly I don't."

"I mean, how to have a fun life, without slaving away in an office somewhere. One way, one option, was to marry some-body with a billion dollars. Well, to be honest, I'd settle for a lot less. . . . A hundred million, I'd consider it. Just joking. Still, it would be nice. You know, I actually tried. I went on line, it was a kind of ad, you know, in those websites, the ones where all the losers look for sex partners—I know, that's not what they say they're doing. Anyway: my thing said something like this: 'Wanted: a very rich woman, preferably under 40. I'm good-looking, intelligent, lots of fun, good at games, good at sex; I don't smoke or do drugs. Looking for a life partner. Send me a picture.'"

I had to laugh at this. "What happened, Sebastian?"

"You wouldn't believe the weirdos who responded. Nobody the least bit suitable. You'd think they'd appreciate how honest I was. I guess they thought it was a joke. I got one response, actually, that seemed at least possible. She sent me a picture that was at least 20 years old; I had coffee with her, and she was 60 if she was a day. She told me she was good in bed. I never gave her a chance to prove it. She paid for the coffee. I gave up after that. Then there was the second option. . . ."

"What was that, Sebastian?"

"My own family. So near and yet so far. Remember, I had a grandma who was stinking rich. Well, now she's dead, and there's Uncle Morris; and he's stinking rich. I was hoping to get something from Grandma, but it turned out I was wasting my time. Anyway, she was no fool, the old bag—she saw right through me. Then there was Morris. I told him my story, but of course he paid no attention. He actually thought I was joking. I said, Uncle Morris, I don't want to work for a living. You didn't, after all; and look at you now. That's my ambition, to be like you."

"What did he say?"

"He got annoyed. Of course I knew it would be a long shot. Even if he wanted to do something for the family, the old skinflint wouldn't just single me out. He had no sense of humor, of course. Just as bad as his mother. He told me in no uncertain terms that I was a worthless, spoiled brat, of course I agreed with him, I said, yes I am, but I'm family; and he said that anyway he *had* worked for a living, he took care of his old mother, and if I didn't think that was a worthwhile job, well, blah blah; and he said, exactly what did *I* do to justify sitting on my butt doing nothing and I just shrugged my shoulders, and said, OK, Uncle, I just thought I might ask, no harm done."

"All's well that ends well," I said. "Since you're going to get some money. Quite a lot in fact. It's only a one-ninth share, but even so, after taxes, I think the estate will be, oh, maybe 25 or 30 million, and you can do the math yourself."

"You see," he said, grinning from ear to ear. "I told you I was a suspect. I had a real motive for killing him. A couple of million—hey, there's a motive, Frank."

"But he told all of you he was disinheriting you," I said.

"Yeah, but he was lying. . . . And maybe I knew that. Don't ask me how. Maybe we found the will, in his condo. So there's your motive, Frank. Me and the rest of us."

"To be honest, Sebastian," I said, "I don't see you as a killer."

"You think I don't have the guts? You're right. I don't. But who did? I keep racking my brains for suspects. Not about Grandma, that's another story. But about Uncle Morris. I keep coming back to my sister Julia."

"Sebastian, you're being ridiculous again."

"I know, she seems so unlikely. But isn't that the way it is? I love Agatha Christie, I've read all of her books. I wish she put in some sex, but you can't have everything. I mean, not that it matters, there's enough porn on the web, I don't need Agatha Christie. Anyway, in Agatha Christie, it's always the least likely person, isn't it? Well, who could be more unlikely than Julia?"

"Nobody," I said. "But this isn't Agatha Christie. This is life."

"Well, truth is stranger than fiction, isn't that what they say? Did you know that Julia was in the building, you know, where Morris lived, the day he died? She went to see him, God knows why. She wouldn't tell me. She was there in the morning. And then she went back later that day. Just before Aunt Anna did. Maybe there were in it together, the two of them. I said to Julia, this is very suspicious, my dear, what were you doing there? She got all huffy. I was visiting a relative, she said, my uncle; why is that suspicious? I said, you know darn well why. None of us could stand him. So we weren't going to drop in for a social call, right? But I couldn't get another word out of her."

Could he be right? What were they doing there, that day, Julia and Anna? I knew it was none of my business, but I decided to talk to Julia. It was against my better judgment, but since when does one's better judgment really make a difference? I had an excellent excuse: Julia was one of the heirs, and she had already asked me a few questions about the probate process. They were all of them eager for some money—that was only natural. So I made an arrangement to talk to her. Julia had a job—she was an administrative assistant, of some sort, at a software company, Koolstuff, founded by two sixteen year old boys, one of them a Russian immigrant. The company was three years old and was either on the verge of bankruptcy or a sale to Google for billions; I wasn't sure which, and neither, apparently, was Julia.

Not that I expected much from this conversation. Basically, I thought we were at a dead end. Nobody, including the police for all I knew, was any closer to solving the strange case of Morris Gross. And then there was Bertha Gross—but only Sebastian and I, as far as I know, were aware of *this* case too.

A dead end: But then something happened. Johnny Mills, Everett's son, had a hiking accident, and that changed the whole tenor of the case.

16

I heard about the accident from Felicity, who called me with the news. "Julia had this big scare. Her boyfriend, you know, Johnny Mills, had some kind of accident. But he's OK."

"Accident? Car accident?"

"No. He was hiking, and I guess he fell, steep trail I think. He was by himself, so for a while he was missing—but they found him, and he's in pretty good shape."

I thought nothing more about this; I barely knew Johnny— I had only met him once. So I was surprised when he called me, asked to see me, and came limping into my office, on crutches.

"Sorry to hear about your accident," I said.

"Thanks. But I need your advice. My dad told me to come talk to you."

"Advice? What kind of advice?"

"Well, sort of legal advice."

That was surprising. "Legal advice? Why don't you ask your dad, he's a lawyer, remember?"

He said: "Sure. He is. A lawyer. But this is . . . well, I better tell you my story. We had gone camping, you know, it was going to be an overnight thing; me and my father. And Julia, she came along, and some friend of hers. We had two tents. Anyway, we were in this county park up in the hills. Real wild, you know, trails, pretty steep in some places. It was late after-noon. I went off by myself. The rest of them, they'd had enough for the day, but I still had some energy, and I followed the trail, I had a backpack on, and I started climbing up the trail; it was pretty steep. Then, I had to urinate, you know, it happens, and I went off the trail to do it, behind some bushes; and somehow, I tripped, and I went tumbling down this ravine, I couldn't stop myself, all the way down. So there I was, kind of at the bottom, and my leg was killing me, and I couldn't move. Wow, I thought, I'm in trouble, and I had a cell phone, but it didn't work, I guess there's no reception in that kind of place. Honest to God, I thought I was going to die down there. I was scared to death. . . . You know, there's even mountain lions in those hills . . . and it gets so chilly at night. . . . And pretty soon, it was dark, and my leg was bothering me, and I thought, this is a real problem. I had nothing to eat. I had some trail mix in my backpack, but I couldn't reach it, I was kind of immobilized. . . . I had a canteen attached to my belt, so I could drink some water. . . . Anyway, I was there all night."

"That's terrible, Johnny," I said. "Sounds like a real ordeal. I'd be scared to death. But obviously, they came and rescued you."

"Yeah, in the morning. I was in a lot of pain. Couldn't sleep. I tried yelling, but of course that was no use, who would hear me. Jesus, I thought I was a goner, I really did. But then my dad came with some people. What happened was, when I didn't come back and it was night time, they got alarmed. He hiked out, with Julia, and they reported it to somebody and a search party was organized. I don't remember much about it, but they came and hauled me out, police I think, rangers, in the morning, when you could see better, and I was kind of groggy. Julia was with my dad, she was crying, and she said, oh Johnny, I thought you were dead, and Dad had called my mom, his ex-wife, and there was a whole fuss, but it turned out, my leg wasn't broken, just badly sprained, and I'm going to be OK. So that part's all right. But then the trouble started. . . ."

"Trouble?"

"It was my backpack. . . . The police, the rangers, whatever, they found a gun in the backpack, and some other stuff, a paper bag, with some junk in it. They started asking me a bunch of questions, not that day, I was kind of out of it, but the next day; I was home, felt like shit, and I had to go to the doctor, orthopedist, they took X-rays, well, nothing was broken, I told you that, but the leg was sprained, and they wanted me on crutches. Anyway, the police, they asked me, this bag, they asked, where did you get it, and I said, well, it was down there, right where I fell, somebody tossed it I guess. Plain brown bag, like you get in a grocery store. I said, what was inside of it? They didn't believe me when I said I just found it and picked it up and put it in my backpack, in case somebody lost it."

I asked: "And was that true?"

"No way. That was a total lie. I couldn't even reach my backpack. I don't know if they realized that, but anyway, how could I pick up this bag; and the whole story must have sounded like a bunch of crap, which it was. No, the bag was there, in my backpack, all the time. That's why I'm here. I need your advice. Not just legal advice but . . . you see, when they looked inside, and they saw a gun, well, that gun got them all suspicious, and inside the bag was all this broken stuff, like dishes, pottery, all in pieces. And, I don't know how they know this, but they found out somehow, maybe from Anna, or Julia, that it was stuff that had been taken from the condo, you know, where Morris Gross lived, and how did I get it, and so on. They didn't believe my story. I have to admit, I wouldn't believe it either."

Nor would I. It was just too much of a coincidence. There are over 30,000,000 people in California, millions of them in the Bay Area; to believe that Johnny, who had connections with the Gross family, would fall into a ravine at precisely the point where a bag of stuff taken from Morris's condo just happened to be lying around: that simply wasn't believable.

"So what kind of advice do you want, Johnny? Your dad is as good a lawyer as I am; you know that."

"But he's not investigating this case. . . ."

That thing again. The rumor that pursued me; and that I simply couldn't ever get rid of. "Look, Johnny: I am not investigating anything. Whatever rumors you might have heard, they're just not true. I'm a lawyer, period. Not a detective. Not even an amateur detective."

I don't know if I convinced him or not. He said nothing for a while; and then he said, "OK, maybe I believe you. Still, what would you do, in my situation? You see my problem."

"I guess I'd tell the truth. Which is what?"

"OK, I'll tell you," he said. "First of all, I really had an accident, these crutches aren't a joke. I was doing a favor for Julia. The idea was, I was to go pretty far into the woods, find a ravine, someplace pretty inaccessible, and dump the bag and the gun there, so nobody would ever find them. But you know, the best laid plans and so on. I tripped and fell, and I couldn't stop until I reached the bottom, and I banged myself up pretty bad; and, you know the rest. But what should I do?"

"And you're asking me? Johnny, how could I help you? I told you, I'm not investigating anything. What do *you* think this is all about? The gun, the broken stuff. Does it have something to do with, well, Morris Gross?"

"Hey, listen, it's none of my business. I'm in this because of Julia. She's sort of my girlfriend. I say 'sort of,' because so far it's pretty one-sided. Anyway, she begged me to do this. Maybe the gun is the one somebody used to kill Morris Gross, I don't know. She didn't say that. In fact, she said it wasn't. And the junk in the bag, broken pieces of stuff, I have no idea why that's important; but I guess it is."

I didn't know what to make of all this. *Was* this the murder gun? The police had it now; and they would find out, I suppose. I know about as much about ballistics as I do about ancient Chinese poetry, in other words, nothing. My house is a gun-free zone; and I hope it stays that way. I thought about the problem for a while, and then I gave Johnny my best advice: do nothing, for the moment. If the police hound you, tell them the truth.

"I can't do that to Julia," he said. "If I tell them the truth, they'll go after her."

I shrugged my shoulders. "Suit yourself," I said. "I told you what to do."

He nodded, and hobbled off on his crutches. I was reasonably sure he had decided not to say a word to the police. At least not a word of truth.

Nobody ever takes good advice. Nobody.

17

Among the people who never take good advice I have to include myself. Celia gives me good advice every day. OK: it's an exaggeration to say I never take it. If she says, don't wear that shirt, I'll do what she says. I obey her in all the little things; and also in the big, implicit things, like marital fidelity. It's the things in the middle where I simply go my own way.

The next evening, I was chatting after dinner with Celia, telling her about the events of recent days. This included telling her the full story that Johnny told me. "Frank," she said. "I hope you're not spending a lot of time on this thing, you know what I mean."

I did know what she meant, but I pretended I didn't.

"You should manage the estate, naturally; after all, that's your job," she said. "But on the question, who killed Morris Gross? Stay out of it, Frank. It's enough that he's dead, and you're going to see to it that everything goes smoothly, I mean, taxes, the will, all of that. Let the police find out who killed the guy. Not you, Frank. How often do I have to tell you these things? I mean, really."

"But, honey, I've got a duty toward the estate. The law of California, you know, the probate code, that's our Bible; it's very clear—if you kill somebody, you can't inherit. So, in a way, I've got to know if any of the heirs had anything to do with this."

Celia gave me a clear, harsh look. "Frank, that's total rubbish. You're talking yourself into something. The police will decide who killed Morris Gross, not some random member of the California bar who happens to be representing the estate. I mean it: stay out."

I knew she was right. And her warnings would be even sharper and more emphatic, if she knew I was concerned about the death of Bertha Gross as well as the death of Morris Gross. Somehow, in my cowardice, I had never filled her in on that little mystery. I could imagine the withering contempt she would express, if I told her about Morris's little visit to heaven . . . and the fact that, in one sense at least, I took it seriously. Of course, I knew that, eventually, I would have to let her know about Morris's excursion to heaven. I couldn't keep it a secret forever. Twenty years of marriage have to count for something.

I had arranged an appointment to talk to Julia Gross. My excuse—and it was not completely dishonest—was that Julia was an heir, and I needed to talk to her about the estate. Of course, I had an ulterior motive. I wanted to know more about the gun and the broken crockery. I was pretty sure what the broken crockery meant: these were remains of some of Morris's gewgaws, which somebody—Julia perhaps?—had stolen from the house, either before or after Morris's death. Why they were stolen, and how they got broken, was still a mystery.

Maybe they were, or had been, extremely valuable. This well-known program on the air, "Antiques Roadshow," is a show in which people trot out hideous gimcracks from their basements and attics, show them to a gaggle of smooth, self-satisfied experts, and find out they have a rare chamber pot from the time of Victoria, or an old wooden chair with legs shaped like bird-claws, items which (according to the experts) are worth some amazing amount of money. A sum which I'm sure they could never get from an actual antique dealer, who would have to turn around and sell the wretched thing to a customer at a profit. I think the program appeals to people the way the lottery does. Maybe Grandma's teapot will bring me untold riches. Or maybe this landscape of Yosemite or this dish that I bought at a garage sale. I'm sure what most people bring to the show is worthless junk, and they are quickly disillusioned. But the producers suppress most of that, I guess. They only show us the winners, the surprises. What, this cane with a silver handle is really worth thousands of dollars? Who would have guessed?

Julia was an attractive woman, with soft brown hair. She had bland, regular features, and she talked in a soft voice. She seemed quiet and reserved: the kind of person that, well, you never really know what goes on in their mind. The exact opposite of her brother Sebastian.

After we did our estate business, I gingerly broached the topic I was really concerned with. "Your friend Johnny was here the other day."

She looked at me, warily. I went on: "He told me all about his accident. That must have been scary for you."

"It was."

"He wanted advice, Julia. Do you know what about?"

"Not really," she said. "Tell me."

I told her. "He admitted, his story was a lie; but of course I knew that. I think the police must know that too. I know it's none of my business, but he's telling the lie to protect *you*, Julia. He got the bag, the gun, and the crockery from you."

She was quiet for a while. Then she said: "But it's not me he's protecting. I mean, yes, he did it as a favor to me. But it wasn't about me. It was about my Aunt Anna. It was her stuff. I told her I would find a way to get rid of it. I thought about putting it in a dumpster, but I was worried, maybe somebody would find the gun and that could lead to trouble. I thought about tossing the stuff in the Bay or something like that, but I was afraid to do that. I asked Johnny to help me. He volunteered to do it. Look, he said, we're going on this hike, you and I, and your friend Mavis, and my dad. Really remote place, you know, total wilderness. I'll find some ravine, some place off the trails, some place where nobody will ever find it, and I'll dump it there. That was the plan. Unfortunately, poor Johnny had this accident, and . . . well, you know the rest."

"It was Anna's gun?"

"Well, her late husband had it, I guess. But yes, it was her gun. Don't get any wrong ideas, though. The police tested it right away. It wasn't the gun that killed Uncle Morris. I guess Aunt Anna doesn't know much about guns, I don't either, and she just felt it might look suspicious, I mean, her having this gun at all, and. . . . Anyway, that's the truth."

"And the broken stuff? In the brown bag?"

"That was stuff from Uncle Morris's house. Aunt Anna took these things. She shouldn't have done that. But she did. She took a bunch of small things, figurines, I'm not sure what else. She felt she had a right to have them."

"But this stuff was broken?"

"Well . . . yes, it was. She smashed three of them, three of the things she took. One was a soapstone vase, with sort-of flowers on it; and another one, in the shape of some animal, an elephant, I think; and the third was a little porcelain thing, a shepherdess."

"She smashed them? Why did she do that?"

"I honestly don't know. Maybe she just dropped them, accidentally. Or maybe not. The other stuff she took, she brought back, put back in the apartment. You know she has a key. But these three, she couldn't, because they were in pieces. But the police don't seem the least bit interested in the broken stuff. And they're not valuable, as far as I know."

"Then why was she so anxious to get rid of this junk?"

"I don't know. Probably because she didn't want the police to know she had been in the place, and taken stuff. Aunt Anna and I are pretty close, she tells me things. She came to me, she was all excited, all upset, and she said she had taken some items out of the condo. Like I said, she had a key. She wasn't supposed to, but she had one anyway."

"Was she there, in the apartment, *after* he died?"

"I can't talk about that. I really can't. She was there maybe the next day. Don't ask me about that. Frank, I have to tell you, Aunt Anna went through her brother's papers. I don't know exactly when, but she did. She found the new will, and she took it. When she read it, and saw that we were all going to get the money, she put it back."

"And did she take something else, an envelope?"

"What kind of envelope?"

"I don't know," I said. "Just an envelope. Your uncle left me a letter, and in that letter, he said he put a message in another envelope. But we never found that envelope. Did your aunt take that too?"

"She never said anything about an envelope. And I never saw that letter."

But I had. And I had read—and written—the older wills. I knew about the list of gewgaws. The list of what, as I said, we lawyers call specific bequests. I wish I had that envelope; but clearly it was gone, and I felt we would never see it. Who took it? Maybe the person who killed Uncle Morris.

Could that be Anna? His own sister? That idea had popped into my mind from time to time, only to be rejected. She just did not seem like a killer. Especially a brother-killer and a mother-killer. But her behavior was certainly suspicious.

As soon as Julia left, I went over my files. I pored over every scrap of information, every note, every draft, that dealt with Morris Gross. Mostly, I came up with nothing that pointed toward a solution to the mystery. With one exception. The list of specific bequests.

I was beginning, vaguely, to formulate . . . something. I had a feeling, a gut feeling, about the murder of Morris Gross. I told myself: stop thinking about this. Let the police do their work. I could hear Celia's voice giving me that advice—again. It was as if she had recorded her advice, and implanted it just under my skin.

But Johnny's story, and Julia's—that made a difference. And soon I would hear another voice talking, feeding me information.

It was an unexpected visit from Everett Mills. And it opened up a whole new can of worms.

18

I hadn't expected to see Everett Mills, and when he called me, I thought it must be about some client of his, or of mine. We agreed to meet for lunch in Redwood City, near the courthouse, where he had business, he said. Redwood City is the county seat of our county (San Mateo). The city itself is a fascinating mixture of Mexican immigrants, with their bodegas, and more affluent citizens, whose houses climb the hills in the western part of the city. The downtown, like all Bay Area downtowns, was full of a bewildering array of ethnic restaurants. You have to wonder if anybody eats at home in California.

I met Everett in a Thai restaurant, of no particular distinction—the usual sort, with the usual menu, and a picture of the king of Thailand smiling from the walls. Everett ordered very little, and ate even less. "I have all these food allergies," he said. "And heartburn. I take pills."

The Thai restaurant had been my idea, mostly because of its location. Perhaps I had made a mistake. In any event, Everett looked worried. He was sweating, even though the restaurant was air-conditioned (and much too cool for my taste). After we put in our orders, he started talking:

"I know my Johnny went to see you the other day. You know, he's in trouble."

"Oh, I know that," I said. "But I think it'll be all right."

"No, no," he said. "You don't understand. It's not just that business with the gun and the broken stuff. You know, by the way, that that gun wasn't the gun that killed Morris Gross. It was a perfectly legal weapon, it was Anna's; she got it from her husband. The police were probably wondering why anybody would throw a gun away, I don't know if that's some kind of offense, well, probably it isn't. Anyway, that's not the problem. It's something else."

"Something else?"

"The police are asking Johnny things. Like, if he could account for his whereabouts, the night Morris was killed."

"Johnny? They suspect Johnny?"

"I hope not. Maybe they suspect me . . . that's what I wanted to talk to you about. I thought I should tell you the whole story. They say you're working on the case; I'm not sure I believe that. . . ."

"Honestly, I'm not."

"OK, OK, but you're handling the estate, and . . . anyway, I just wanted you to know the whole story. I mean, as much of the story as I know myself. The police . . . the detectives . . . or whoever's investigating this, I worry that they have me in their sights."

"You, Everett?" I said. The food arrived, and he was quiet for a moment. I took a forkful of pad Thai. I love pad Thai. Everett stared at his plate. "Why on earth would anybody think such a thing?"

He said. "Well . . . just listen. This all has to do with Bertha. Bertha Gross. The old lady. She was a piece of work, let me tell you. Anyway . . . I was her lawyer, you remember. Drew up the will. I'll be honest with you, Frank, I was hoping she'd die soon. I needed the money desperately. An estate of that size! Wow. For guys like us, that comes along once in a lifetime. It's only human to . . . well, anticipate the money."

I nodded. This came quite close to home. I've mentioned Celia's plans for a new refrigerator, and new tile in the bathroom, and kitchen projects. And my dreams of a trip to Italy

"There's something you don't know," he said. "It has to do with this woman named Jasmine. She was married to Charlie Gross, I suppose you know that."

I did. "She left him for a plumber," I said. "Felicity told me that." I remember that conversation well. She described the plumber in detail. He was young, with dirty blonde hair, she said. He wore little plastic things on his feet. She said "Jasmine, Daddy's wife—I could never bring myself to call her a step-mother—she was always bitching and moaning about everything, including the plumbing. So we had to call a plumber. I let him in the door, and Jasmine was there, and she was all over him, it was disgusting, the minute she laid eyes on him, she said the toilet is clogged, but I'll bet you have a big strong snake that can wriggle down into it and fix it. I mean, she was disgusting, she practically threw herself at him."

"The plumber didn't last long," Everett said. "Jasmine wasn't about to give up her marriage for a plumber. Not while she had a super-rich mother-in-law. That guy was a sex object, that's all. Well, so was she. Frank, what happened next was . . . me. I fell madly in love with her. She was no good, but that didn't matter, Frank. I simply wanted her. After this plumber business, well, it was me and Jasmine."

"These things happen," I said, lamely.

"I felt bad about Charlie," he said. "I mean, he was a client after all. Well, his family was, especially Bertha. But Charlie was history already. Maybe I told myself that the marriage was dead, to make myself feel better. Jasmine told me she hated him. She said she couldn't stand him. He had body odor, she told me. He had hair in his nose."

"Weren't you married?" I asked. "I mean, I'm not passing judgment. . . ."

"I was separated. I'm not good with women, I guess. I was married twice. The first wife, well, that was long ago. Then I married Myrna, and we had Johnny. She left me, I had to raise Johnny myself. Then I met Jasmine. . . . She had moved out, she wasn't with Charlie anymore, she had an apartment. I used to visit her there. I was totally besotted. I couldn't eat and sleep. Here I am, a member of the California bar, a professional, and I was just like some kind of moonstruck teen-ager. I'm disgusted with myself. No wonder Myrna refused to come back. She got a divorce. I don't blame her. But she shouldn't have run out on our son. . . ."

"Things happen," I said again, for want of a better comment.

"So this is how things stood. I was madly in love with Jasmine, but she was Charlie's wife. OK, that marriage was dead, as I told you. But . . . Bertha—that's when she entered the picture. She read me the riot act. She said I was a disgrace, God, Frank, she said all sorts of things. I was there in the condo. She called me up and demanded that I come there to see her. When I got there, I had to put up with her fury. I mean, she was a real bitch, I always knew that."

"Was Morris there?" I asked.

"Morris? I guess he was. Somewhere on the premises. I don't really remember. He must have heard every word though. Anyway, I tried to answer her, I said I was sorry, that Jasmine and I were in love, and that Jasmine was separated from Charlie, I wasn't the first—I didn't break up the marriage and so on. But she wouldn't listen to a word of it. She said, you're carrying on with my daughter-in-law, you're a disgrace to your profession, and I don't want to see you ever again, and she went on and on about people nowadays, in her day things were different, all this sex and infidelity, it was disgusting, blah blah. I had to stand there and take it. For me, Frank, it was a disaster. And she said that as far as she was concerned, I wasn't her lawyer any more. She'd get somebody else, she said. And here I was, counting on her business. . . ."

"You were counting on her business?"

"Don't judge me, Frank. She was 94. She had a huge estate. I needed the money, the fees. I was in debt, Myrna was taking me to the cleaners, and I owed money, I made bad investments. I begged and pleaded with Bertha, I told her I would do anything, but of course I couldn't give up Jasmine, I never said that I would, fool that I was. And I left there totally depressed, and I thought, this is it, I've lost my best client."

"But you didn't lose the client, Everett," I said. "As I recall, you handled the estate."

"Sheer luck, Frank. You see, she died either the next day, or a day and a half later, I don't remember. Never had a chance to get rid of me. I felt guilty, because I knew she'd be whirling in her grave, if she knew I had the business. But I filed the will, the old will, and I proceeded to handle the estate. I told you, I needed the money. I never told anybody about the scene with her, I mean, it was perfectly legal; her will, the one I wrote, the one I probated, well, it had never been revoked, and it said plainly that I was supposed to be the lawyer for the estate. And I did a good job, a professional job. I charged the statutory fees, nothing more, didn't ask for extraordinary fees, like most lawyers do."

"And Morris? He knew, I gather, about the scene between you and his mother."

"He knew. Oh, believe me, he knew. And I thought: he'll fire me. He was such a mama's boy, and he knew she was angry with me. But he didn't fire me. I was surprised: sure, he tried to bargain with me, he wanted me to lower my fees; I wouldn't do that. But why didn't he get another lawyer? I couldn't figure it out. I still can't. Anyway, I saw the estate through, to the end. I didn't get along with Morris, but, I figured, what the hell, I never expected him to die so soon, and I thought, he'll never use me anyway. I mean, whatever money I got out of the estate, believe me, I earned it. Dealing with him, I wouldn't wish it on anybody. He and his mother. They were two of a kind."

"He was difficult. Morris. I know it."

"But then—and this is something I just don't get—a few days before he died, he called me up, and he was absolutely vile over the phone. First of all, he went on about Johnny. As you know, Julia Gross has a crush on him. I don't know if Johnny feels the same way. Me, I like her. She's a nice woman. But getting back to Morris, he was absolutely hateful, he said, he didn't want my son having any sort of relationship with his niece, and he demanded that I break it off. I said, Morris, how can I do that? He said, you figure it out. He said, your son, he just wants my money, but he won't get a penny of it, and so on. You think he's marrying a gold mine. That's what he said, his very words. A gold mine. I said, you don't know Johnny, he's a good boy. But he said, I don't have to leave a penny to Julia, and believe me, I won't. What could I say? I said, Morris, it's your money. You can leave it to the man in the moon, if you want to."

"But he didn't disinherit her after all," I said.

"I guess not," Everett said. "Lady luck again. Somebody killed the bastard. First he told the whole family, he wasn't leaving them a dime, then he changed his mind, and then somebody did him in. Julia's going to be rich. But that's not all," he said, fidgeting slightly. "There's something else."

"Something else?"

"When he got done railing about Johnny, he said, and you, Mr. Lawyer, I'm going to see to it that you're hounded out of the profession. I'm going to tell them that my mother wanted to change her will, and she wanted you out of the picture, you were sleeping with her daughter-in-law, and you had no right to handle the estate. I'll tell that to the authorities. You're in big trouble."

"Of course, that's nonsense," I said. "You didn't do anything wrong."

"Yes, I know that. But he said, he was going to go to the Bar Association, and he was going to do this that and the other thing. Go to the police, too. I mean, he intended to drag my name through the mud. Sure, I didn't do anything wrong. Legally or ethically. She didn't change her will; and sleeping with somebody's niece, hey, if the Bar Association disciplined people for having an affair, we'd have a lawyer shortage in California. But the man was ignorant as well as vile. He was ranting and raving; and what could I do about it. Nothing. I couldn't stop him from complaining to everybody and everything under the sun. He wouldn't get anywhere, but of course it would be bad for me, bad for my career—it could be a nightmare. But, as I said, I was lucky again. Lucky because somebody got rid of him. But unlucky, because, well, the police have been questioning me, and I don't have an alibi. I mean, it's ridiculous, I'm not a murderer. But all this is driving me crazy."

Meanwhile, my mind was racing away. Two lucky deaths. But were they really just dumb luck? Everett Mills was in a way the first person involved in this mess who actually had a motive, not just for killing Morris Gross, but Bertha Gross as well. And Julia? Was she as innocent as she made out? I couldn't imagine her killing her uncle, it just didn't seem in character; still, what do I know? Whose name was on that missing piece of paper? Was it Julia? Did she just take that envelope, and tear it up? Maybe Morris did try to disinherit her—it wouldn't have worked, but he didn't know that. Or was it Everett Mills—was his name on the paper?

"But why," I asked, "after all that happened . . . why did he suddenly turn on you? He didn't make a fuss after his mother died. What made him so angry, after all that time?"

"I honestly don't know. It was damn peculiar. Not a peep out of him for months and months; and then this. Was it Johnny and Julia? Could be. But somehow I don't think so. There was something else. What it was, I have no idea."

Another puzzle. Two lucky deaths, as I said. Was there a third? Charlie Gross was also dead. Did I dare mention it? I asked Everett: "When . . . when did Charlie Gross die? It was an auto accident, wasn't it?"

"What are you thinking, Frank? Another lucky death? For God's sake! Really! He and Jasmine, they hadn't been together for, oh, I don't know how long. Look: I did feel guilty about his death. He crashed his car—maybe it was suicide, who knows? He was dead drunk. But really, if you have to blame somebody, it was those two women—Jasmine, of course, but his mother too. She humiliated him. She was a prudish old bitch, she hated Jasmine, always had, and she went on and on, why did you marry that slut, I told you so. And then, when she found out he still had some sort of sex life, whatever it was, she made his life miserable, threatened to disinherit him, that was one of her favorite tricks. He was drinking heavily. Look: he was a loser. Let's face it. Maybe I am too. Sometimes I think so."

The food was still sitting on his plate. I had polished off all of mine, and was anxious to order dessert, but I thought it would seem callous. Everett said he wasn't hungry, and the waiter cleared his food away. I craved one of their signature desserts, a sort of mango pudding, but I didn't want the man to think I was obsessed with food, at a time when he was spilling his guts out to me. I thought: I'll have the mango pudding next time.

"And you know," he went on, "Jasmine disappeared. Vanished. No note, nothing: just gone. I think maybe they think I killed her, buried the body, or whatever. They ask all sorts of questions. The police. Why would I kill her? I loved her. When I realized she was gone, Frank, I was totally devastated. I couldn't eat, sleep, or work for days. It's still a terrible heartache. I miss her."

"And you have no idea where she is?"

"None at all. . . . I was wondering . . . I was thinking of hiring a detective maybe. . . . Trying to trace her. I do have one good lead."

"What's that?"

"That doctor. Melrose Percival. He was the family doctor; the old lady, Bertha, she had him all the time. She was a bit of a hypochondriac. She used to call him day and night, and he would drop everything and come over. He was sort of the family doctor. That included Jasmine. She went to him a lot. I have to admit, I was jealous. I used to wonder, why did she need to see the doctor all the time? I suspected they were having an affair. I really did. What she could see in an old goat like that, I have no idea. But she was . . . voracious, if you know what I mean."

"And now she's gone."

"Frank, is she alive or dead? I haven't heard a word from her, and it's driving me crazy. Listen: you're working on this case. . . ."

"Everett, believe me, I'm not. Please."

"Look, maybe it's not official, but I know you're trying to figure things out. I heard stuff from Julia, from Sebastian. Sebastian's working for you, isn't he? He has some crazy thing about toothpaste, did you put him up to that?"

"Everett, for God's sakes," I said. "You know Sebastian. He goes off on his own."

"OK, OK, I know that," he said. "Johnny can't stand him, actually. I don't mind Sebastian, I think he's basically harmless; but then again, he can be a pain in the butt. Anyway: what I wanted to say was this: people say, it was somebody in the family, I mean, whoever got rid of Morris Gross. If I were you, I'd check on the doctor. Mel Percival."

"Dr. Percival? But why would he kill Morris Gross?"

"I honestly don't know. But I think he's a dangerous man. Looks so harmless, so . . . medical, if you know what I mean. Calm voice, very professional manner, that sort of thing. You want to know my deepest, darkest suspicion? I think he stole Jasmine from me. And then he killed her."

"Everett," I said, "why would he do that?"

"Money. Everything is money. He thought the old lady would leave him money, maybe. I don't know. But she was so damn disapproving of . . . anything sexual. I told you about *my* situation. Well, if Jasmine was fooling around with the doctor, and she found out, she would have had a cow. And that would be the end of any hope for Dr. Melrose Percival. He could kiss the money goodbye."

I pooh-poohed the idea. I didn't see a real motive for Dr. Percival. Yes, he was a close family friend; but surely he knew better than to expect money from Bertha Gross. But I did begin to wonder. I had no idea whether Dr. Percival had anything to do with the disappearance of this Jasmine woman, who I had never seen. Did he murder Bertha Gross, on the other hand? Morris Gross believed that somebody killed his mother. I knew about that suspicion. Everett Mills did not.

Dr. Melrose Percival: he was there, that last evening, when Bertha Gross took sick, mysteriously, and died in her sleep, or in an ambulance; in any event, she was dead before morning. I thought the idea of poisoned toothpaste was ridiculous; but the idea of some other kind of poison, something to ease Bertha Gross into another world, that was not so ridiculous. Doctors do that all the time. Mercy killing. Only this would have been something different. Merciless in fact.

Is this what Morris Gross heard in heaven? An accusation against Dr. Percival?

What *did* happen that night, at the old lady's house? I was consumed with curiosity. Maybe Morris's message didn't come from heaven; but there must have been something behind it. I had to find a reason to talk to Dr. Percival. But what?

19

Fate stepped in. Or rather, Sebastian. He called me on the phone, somewhat breathlessly. "Frank," he said, "I need to give you a progress report."

I doubted whether Sebastian was making any progress; or could possibly be making progress. But I agreed to see him. That afternoon, he appeared in my office, wearing a bright blue T-Shirt, with the words "Open for Business" emblazoned on them. "I'm going to start a company," he said. "You need money to start a business, but I'm getting money from Uncle Morris, isn't that true?"

"Absolutely, Sebastian."

"I've got this great idea, Frank. Just listen. A sperm donor company. I know, we have those already. But my company, it's going to be different. We're going after single women, you know, women who want babies, but the clock is ticking. Good-looking women, sexy women, no husbands—but they're dying to be mothers, women always want to be mothers, don't they? I mean, it's evolution, right? Anyway, the idea is, these guys will have sex with the women, they sign away the babies, the sex is just for fun, but the women get pregnant, which is what they want. So they get the sperm, and have fun meanwhile. What do you think? No more turkey basters. We offer the real thing, real sex, but no strings attached."

"And who are these guys?"

"Well, me for one. But I'll get others. Real studs. Young guys. Athletes. Guys that like sex, and who doesn't, you know? I'll screen the women. No fatties. They've got to pass a test, good looks, no diseases. The guys the same. What do you think, Frank? Can you handle the legal end?"

"The legal end? I suppose so," I said. Not that I expected anything to come of this scheme. Sebastian probably had this sort of impulse every once in a while, a revelation of sorts, but I would hazard a guess that he was weak on follow-through.

"Also," he said. "I've been working on the case. Maybe, if my business model doesn't work, I'll become a private detective. Nothing dangerous, but, you know, spying on guys, are they cheating, that line of work? You can be my partner, Frank."

I told him no thanks.

"Whatever. Anyway, my uncle's case. I've got a lot of ideas. I've narrowed it down to two people. One is Aunt Anna. I mean, she had motive, she had opportunity, she had a gun, lots of reasons. But then I decided, no, she's out."

"Oh, really? And why is that?"

"Frank, she's family. I mean, she practically raised me. My mom died when I was an infant, and this Jasmine, I swear, why Charlie ever married her, it's a mystery; and why she married him, God only knows. Must have been something about money. Anyway, she was no mother-figure, I mean, she was more likely waiting for me to reach puberty so she could take my virginity. That's the kind of woman she was. Never mind. Aunt Anna. I mean, she can be a pain in the butt, but she loved me, and she took care of me, so I just can't go around saying she murdered people, now, can I? I talked to Julia about this, I said, maybe it's Aunt Anna, and she burst into tears, she said I was awful, so that's the end of that. Aunt Anna is out."

"Sebastian, that's hardly a reason."

"Well, it is for me. And the toothpaste, I'm not getting anywhere. It's a long shot. What we needed was the missing tube, you know? So they could analyze it in a lab. Anyway, I'm looking for somebody outside the family. Mel Percival. He's the one. That's my latest idea. The doctor. I never liked him anyway."

"Sebastian," I said, "that's no reason either. You're saying he's a murderer because, first, he's not a relative, and second, you don't like him."

"He was always hanging around the house, you know? What was he doing there? I mean, they weren't that sick. He used to drop in on Uncle Morris. He was there a lot, the week before Morris got it in the neck. I know he was there. Millicent Whetstone, she saw him. She's next door, she sees who comes and goes. I mean, not that she's spying on him or that sort of thing. But if she's going in and out, and somebody's going in and out at Uncle Morris's, well, she sees him."

"OK," I said. "But is that all?"

"Family gossip," he said. "The guy was doing it with Jasmine. I mean, I think she'd sleep with a gorilla in the zoo, if nothing else was available. My father was a damn fool; anyway, she ditched him, can't say it broke my heart; she was doing it with Johnny's father, and some plumber, and God knows who else. Probably Mel Percival. I think he killed her, by the way. She went to his office, and she disappeared. I think she never came out. Doctors, they know how to kill people. Sometimes they kill people without meaning to. But sometimes they do it on purpose. Give you pills. Or inject something, like, here's a shot, it's a painkiller, that's what they say—but it's not a painkiller, it's something else, and boom, you're dead. I read about that someplace. Anyway, I don't know what he did with the body, there's that problem; but still, she went in to his office, and nobody's seen her since."

"Sebastian, you're just making wild guesses. Frankly, I don't care about this Jasmine woman, dead or alive."

"But isn't it funny, how this doctor guy turns up, and then somebody dies? I mean, he hangs around, and everybody in the family dies. This Jasmine, I mean, suppose she's dead? Melrose Percival, he's the last to see her. Next, he's hanging around Grandma, and she's dead—and now Uncle Morris. I mean, it can't be a coincidence. I'm dying to know what kind of toothpaste he uses. OK, OK, let's forget the toothpaste. He wouldn't tell me, anyway."

"You asked him?"

"I did. Yes. I asked him. I said I was working for a company, part-time job, marketing, some sort of shit, I don't think he believed me for a minute. I said, we're taking a survey. What kind of toothpaste do people use? He said, Sebastian, what on earth are you up to? But then I guess he talked to Aunt Anna, or Julia, I don't know which one, and he called me back, and he said, he never heard anything so crazy in his life. I mean, the toothpaste idea. He said, it was just plain impossible; but I don't believe him. Why couldn't you put poison in toothpaste? But then he said, did I honestly think he killed Uncle Morris?"

"So what did you tell him, Sebastian?"

"Promise you won't be mad."

"Oh God. Sebastian, what did you say?"

"I said I was working for you. You were investigating the case. You're handling the estate. Well, you and Felicity, but I left that part out. It was your duty to try to find out, who killed Uncle Morris. And you asked me to help you. Well, that was sort of a lie, Frank. But I hope you don't mind."

"Sebastian," I said, trying to control myself. "I do mind. I very much mind. You have absolutely no right to go around saying such things."

"Hey, I said I was sorry. And isn't part of it true? I mean, you *are* working on the case."

"Sebastian, I am not, repeat not, working on the case. Please. Give me a break. And when did this happen, when did you tell this story to Dr. Percival."

"Yesterday. I think you're going to hear from him. I wanted to warn you. I'm sorry. But," he said, with a big fat smile on his face, "be honest, Frank, it's exciting, isn't it? And I really do think, this guy did it. You can't trust doctors, can you?"

I was speechless.

20

Despite everything, I couldn't help liking Sebastian. He was outrageous, he was causing mischief, and yet there was something about him that I liked. He was floating through life on a raft of charm and guile, but the guile was utterly transparent, and the charm was real. I was, to be honest, furious with him for a while; but then I calmed down.

I have no notion what he intends to do with his life, aside from the crazy schemes he dreams up; and how he will go about making a living. Of course, he is the sort of person who could be successful selling vacuum cleaners door to door. He might even like the job; he'd meet all sorts of people, including desperate housewives. Sebastian was a people person, as he himself said. He would do great at certain kinds of job. If he felt like working, that is.

But of course the work ethic was not Sebastian's thing. I doubted that he would want to sell vacuum cleaners. And, after all, he was going to inherit a nice chunk of money. Though I did wonder how long the money would last.

I thought about all these things, at dinner. My older daughter brought a friend over, of the male species; she said they were working on a project for Advanced Placement History. He was skinny, and wore a T-shirt and baggy pants, which drooped low enough on his hips for the world to see the tops of his underwear, replete with orange and purple stripes. He had traces of acne, and the rather pathetic beginnings of a moustache. He was, of course, sullen. Like my daughter, he treated me and Celia as if we were creatures from another planet. His name, I was told, was Jared. His parents were divorced.

Well, Jared was bright, I suppose—he was in advanced placement courses, after all. For all I know, he would grow up to win a Nobel Prize. It was not impossible. Which was more than you could say for Sebastian.

Sebastian, bless him, was the source of the phone call that came to the house shortly after dinner was over, and the dishes were piled in the sink. The caller was Dr. Melrose Percival. He said: "Mr. May, I believe there are things we ought to talk about. You heard from Sebastian Gross, didn't you?"

"Yes, Doctor, I did." We dickered about a time to get together. Dr. Percival was, like most doctors, a pretty busy man. He had a regular day job, his position in internal medicine at the clinic. "I don't work on Thursdays, though," he said. "I'm nearing retirement age, and I'm slacking off."

We met on Thursday, in the afternoon. Percival was tall and thin, with a tiny white moustache, long hands, and a hooked nose; he was slightly stooped. "I've decided to quit the practice," he said. "I'm over 60. Life is too short to go on working the way I do. And nowadays, the red tape, the paper work, it's killing us. I'm going to travel for a while. Then work on my hobbies. Watercolors. And piano. I'm going to practice four hours a day. I love to play."

I asked him about his relationship with the Gross family. "That was moonlighting," he said. "The old man had been a patient. After he died, I was Bertha's doctor. She hated doctors, actually. Thought they were essentially fraudulent; but somehow she trusted me. She refused to come to the clinic; I had to go to her house; and I did. At first, I used to send her a bill, but then, since she never paid me, I just forgot about it. I wrote it off as charity."

"Charity?" I said. "She was a very rich woman."

"I was being sarcastic," he said. "We became, well, friends. Sort of. I mean, how could you be friendly with her? She was a difficult, stubborn old woman. And Morris, he was much the same. The rest of the family, they were different. They were my patients, too; but they came to the clinic, and they paid their bills. Even Jasmine."

"She's disappeared," I said. "That's what Everett Mills told me."

"What else did he tell you? That I killed her? Sebastian must have said that too. That boy has a vivid imagination. He asked me what kind of toothpaste I used. I said, what for? He said he was conducting a survey. Of course he was lying. I asked Julia, she's more sensible. It's some cockeyed thing about poisoned toothpaste. Ridiculous. And the whole Jasmine thing is ridiculous, too."

"What I heard was, she was last seen entering your office; and never seen since."

"My office is in a clinic; in a three-story building. There's a hundred doctors, two hundred nurses, and God knows how many receptionists, janitors, and aides. Yes, she was seen entering my office. But then she left. The place is busy, there's always people around; how on earth could I have killed a patient and hidden the body? It just doesn't happen. That boy has a vivid imagination. Anyway, as far as the Gross family is concerned, the woman disappeared off the face of the earth. It happens, though, that I know exactly where she is."

"She isn't dead?"

"Not as far as I know. Those rumors are absolute rubbish. She came to see me, yes, and I examined her. The woman was pregnant. God knows who the father was. I was in my office at the clinic, as I told you. I examined her, we talked about the pregnancy, I recommended an obstetrician. She left. I saw more patients; and then went home. That's all."

"And you never saw her after that?"

"No, I never did. I'm pretty sure she had an abortion. At least that's what she told me. She called me later on, and that was the story. I think it was the plumber's baby, but who knows? You know, the family hates her; OK, she was promiscuous, but she wasn't a bad person. And all this stuff about her disappearing—that's rubbish too. She's living in a cabin in Maine, with a gas-meter reader, although who knows how long he'll last. But she's OK, she isn't dead. You can forget all about her."

I crossed her off my mental list.

"Sebastian says you're working hand in glove with the police, trying to figure out who killed Morris Gross," he said. "He also told me I was a prime suspect, can you imagine? I hope you're not spreading that kind of rumor. I'd be furious if you were. But Sebastian—well, you know Sebastian—he's capable of saying anything. I'd like you to put the record straight."

"I'd be happy to," I said. "You're right about Sebastian. I mean, not to believe anything he says. In the first place, I'm not really investigating anything. And I'm not spreading any rumors, about you or anybody else."

"I'm glad to hear that. But I want to straighten something else out, too. Sebastian told me that his uncle, the old fool, told him some crazy story about dying and going to heaven and coming back. And that his mother said something to him in heaven, about somebody killing her or the like. Sebastian also said there was only one other person who knows that ridiculous story, and that's you."

"Yes, that's true. Morris did tell me that story. About dying and going to heaven, and coming back."

"And you believed him?"

"No, of course not. Not for a second. But, you know, he really thought it happened, and I suppose people who are in intensive care, and getting all sorts of drugs and medicines, maybe they hallucinate. Anyway, I don't go around calling clients liars. Not rich ones, anyway."

"Look: I was the family doctor. He had a massive heart attack. Nearly died, and it was touch and go for a while. But then he rallied. I can assure you he was never dead enough to go to heaven, assuming there is such a place, which I don't really believe. I came to the hospital every day. I know the whole medical story. I don't doubt that he had some sort of dream, or vision, or his subconscious told him a story. But he wouldn't be the first or the last. All sorts of people claim they have out-of-body experiences. But no, he didn't die and go to heaven. And, as far as that story is concerned, I can assure you, nobody murdered his mother. I was there the night she died."

"But, OK, Mel, so she just died a natural death. I can believe that; she was really old, and her time was bound to come. But why would he *think* somebody killed her? And who did he suspect? He never told me."

"Of course he wouldn't tell you. Because he suspected himself."

"Himself?"

"Yes, didn't you know that? The minute I heard about this story, I realized what Morris was saying, and why he was saying it. It was plain old-fashioned guilt. He felt he was responsible, that he killed her, and that's why, when he thought he saw her, up in heaven, and she said her spirit was troubled, and all that nonsense, the guilt was overpowering. Then, when he asked her, why was her spirit troubled, she told him it was because he had killed her. You can imagine how he felt."

"But why would he feel that he had killed his mother? You're saying he didn't kill her, aren't you?"

"Exactly. Not literally, at any rate."

"Then why feel guilty?"

"Two reasons. One of them I know all about. The other is still a bit mysterious. That night, I was there, and she said she wasn't feeling well, and went to bed. Actually, I hadn't seen her. When I came, that's what Morris told me; she was already in bed. Other people came, too: Morris's sister, his niece, and the accountant. That was strange. Why was the accountant there? And then this lawyer came, Everett Mills. Bertha had called the two of them, God knows why, but of course they couldn't talk to her. Then I took Morris aside, and I said, do you want me to look in on your mother, if she's sick? But he said, no, no, it wasn't that way at all; she just didn't want to see anybody, and they had had some kind of quarrel, and she was terribly upset. He said that Bertha was absolutely furious with him, Morris, she would never forgive him, and he started blubbering and sobbing and carrying on. I said, Morris, get a grip on yourself, what's this all about? But he wouldn't tell me."

"And you still don't know?"

"I don't. I went home, then. But an hour later, he called me, and he was pretty hysterical, and he said, it's Mother, I can't wake her. I rushed over. She had had a massive heart attack, and it was pretty clear she was going, she was in bad shape, but she was still breathing. He said, call an ambulance, do something. I said, Morris, your mother is 94, she can't survive this, I'll call an ambulance, but believe me, it's no use. Just let her go. He was completely beside himself, he kept saying it was all his fault. He went on and on, how he had killed her. I said, nonsense, what do you mean, she's had a heart attack, you had nothing to do with it—but he was blubbering and saying, I've been a bad son, and I said, Morris, get a grip on yourself. You've been a wonderful son. Nobody could have been so devoted. I've been expecting this, frankly, your mother's very old, she's been in failing health."

"What did he say?"

"He kept repeating, no, no, she was strong, she could have lived, this is all my fault. He was so insistent, that I asked him, well, what do you mean? You didn't poison her or beat her, so what can you be talking about? And he said, I can't tell you, it's too awful. And he went on and on, Mother, Mother, and so on. I grabbed him and said, look: it's her time. We all have to die. Just let her go. And he kept talking about getting an ambulance, and so on, and I said, sure, let's get the ambulance. He said, maybe they can save her. I doubted it, but I wasn't going to argue; and he kept saying, I don't know what to do. Then he did something peculiar. He said, give me a minute; and he left the room. I thought this was really strange. He came back after about five minutes. I think he made a phone call. I can't be sure. And then he said to me, in a funny tone of voice, All right. You're right. He sat down, cried a little, and then he called 911. I think she died in the ambulance. The poor man was beside himself. So, Frank, you see, you're barking up the wrong tree: nobody actually killed his mother; but the poor guy thought he did. He did something that upset her, I suppose. They had some kind of quarrel, right before her heart attack, and that made him feel terrifically guilty."

It made sense. I felt this conversation had been terribly helpful. But what on earth was this quarrel about? The one between Morris and his mother. I needed time to think.

"Morris told me," the doctor said, "that I just didn't understand. What didn't I understand, Morris, I asked him? He said: I think I wanted her dead. I said, that's natural Morris, she was very old, she was becoming a burden; she was difficult. You loved her, but at the same time, you had these thoughts. It's only natural. It's very common, I've seen it over and over again, people with very old, very frail parents, some of them with Alzheimer's—that's a nightmare. They come to really resent the old folks, because of the burden. They have no life. He said, no, no, she wasn't a burden. But I wanted her dead. I loved her, but I wanted her dead."

"But why?"

"He refused to say, and frankly, I don't have a clue. But you see, that explains the heaven business. His guilty conscience was speaking. I'm not a psychiatrist, but you don't have to be a psychiatrist, it's clear what he was going through. He felt guilty, he thought he should have done something to save his mother. Of course, that's completely irrational. She was dying. Or he thought that he shouldn't have upset her. Poor guy must have been tortured by the thought. I've seen that before. A guy quarrels with his old dad, then the dad dies two days later, and the son thinks, if only I hadn't said those harsh words, or things like that. But there you are. The point is: nobody killed her. I think he finally understood. He called me, a few days before he died, I'm not sure exactly when; he wanted to talk about this foundation thing, the one that I was supposed to run. And we got to talking, a real conversation, a serious conversation. The only reason he was doing this was the guilt. And this time, I was forceful enough, I guess, I think maybe I convinced him. Maybe that cured him of the guilt. As you know, he dropped that foundation idea."

I thanked the good doctor for coming. He had clarified a whole raft of things. He had cleared up at least part of the mystery. "Still," I said, "somebody killed Morris. And I guess we're still in the dark about that."

He said, "I know it wasn't me, but that's about all. I have no idea who it could be."

"And do you have any idea why he would tell me a lie—why he told me he was going out of town, when he wasn't. That's the excuse he gave me, for not signing his will. But he never went anywhere."

"Not a clue," he said, shaking his head. He had nothing more of interest to say; and soon afterwards he left. I sat in my chair for a while, thinking about all the things I had learned. About what I knew, and what I didn't know.

I was doing exactly what I claimed I wasn't doing: trying to solve the case. Trying to put all the pieces together. Not that I wanted to lend any credence to the idea that I was some sort of great detective. Of course I wasn't. Personally, I'm not even a fan of mystery stories. I hardly ever read them. Except on airplanes, when we're off to visit Celia's family in Jersey City, New Jersey, or flying to Hawaii for a vacation. I can't read anything serious on airplanes; and the movies never appeal to me. I have to admit I like these books, at least on airplanes. Things like Agatha Christie. They can be really clever, you know, the twists at the end. They always fool me

I have nothing in common with the detectives in the pages of those books. And yet: I've been lucky at times—there've been times when the answers seem to fall into my lap. Usually, this is not because I'm Sherlock Holmes. It's because I had inside knowledge. Because I knew the people as people, which the police didn't. Was that true here too? I knew the whole cast of characters. And I was beginning, just beginning to get an idea, about Morris's death. Not because of my little grey cells or any other cells in my brain, or in my liver, pancreas, or anyplace else; but because I had information that nobody else had.

Above all: I knew the list of gewgaws, the list that Morris brought to me, the things he insisted on leaving to particular people. That list was in the will I drafted, but that wasn't his last will; it wasn't the will we filed in court. The list of gewgaws never made it onto the public record. The police knew nothing about this list. But I did. That list, and the fate of those gewgaws—there were real clues there. And of course there was also the toothpaste. That ridiculous toothpaste: but it told a story.

21

I am not an addictive personality, unless a craving for ice cream, french fries, and tortilla chips qualifies as an addiction. But I was definitely addicted to the case of Morris Gross. I was powerless to resist. It was on my mind, as I drove to work, in the mad morning traffic of the Bay Area. I don't have a long commute, but it can be nerve-wracking if you use Highway 101, choked with trucks and solitary drivers fighting traffic on their way to earn their daily bread

I worked on some documents, and then I took a coffee break at the coffee shop I always patronized, down the street. As I sipped my coffee, I did some more thinking. I decided I had been barking up the wrong tree—that most of my hunches had been absolutely wrong. The more I thought about it, the more I was gripped by a new and different hunch. I had a new suspect in mind.

I won't hold out on you. My new focus was on Millicent Whetstone, Morris's neighbor. I had a number of reasons for this suspicion. One small detail stuck out in my mind—the night that Bertha died, Morris Gross had left the room, mysteriously, and was gone for about five minutes. Percival thought he was making a phone call. I think he dashed across the hall, to talk to Millicent Whetstone. Supposedly she hated Morris and he hated her . . .but that could have been an act.

Was there any way I could check on this hunch? Not easily. But I had an idea. I picked up the phone and called Sebastian. It was about ten o'clock. He answered, but groggily; I had obviously interfered with his beauty sleep. "Wow, Frank, why are you calling? It's practically the middle of the night."

"Sebastian, it's ten o'clock. Normal people have been up for hours."

"They can't help it. I can," he said.

"Sebastian," I said, "I need to talk to your girlfriend. Abby Whetstone. She isn't with you, by any chance?"

"Hey, she was. How did you guess? She's not here now. She went to work or something. What do you need to talk to her about?"

"I can't tell you, Sebastian. Trust me on this."

"Is it about Uncle Morris?"

"Yes it is."

"Cool!" he said. "I'll tell her to call you. I'll text her and give her your number."

The minute I put down the phone I regretted what I had done. Celia would consider it completely unforgiveable. But I was into it now, and there was no going back. I had to figure out a strategy. Exactly what did I want to know from Abby? A good lawyer is prepared in advance for depositions, witness testimony, even discussions with a client. I'm afraid I hadn't really prepared myself when, later that day, Abby called me. Her voice was frosty: "What's this all about?"

"I'd rather not say, I mean, not on the phone. Can we meet?"

"Why should I talk to you? Give me a reason."

I took a wild stab. "It's about your mother."

"My mother? You want to talk to me about my mother? Why? And if it's about my mother, why don't you just talk to her?"

"I mean, maybe it's not about your mother," I said, retreating a bit.

"Well, make up your mind. It either is or it isn't. Anyway, I'm busy. Is this something Sebastian dreamed up?"

"No, not really," I said, which wasn't quite true. "It's about something you said . . . to Morris Gross."

"How would you know what I said to Morris Gross, if I said anything?"

Too late I remembered that my source for this information was Sebastian; Abby Whetstone tried to wheedle money out of Morris—that was what Sebastian had said. He said, too, that her weapon was a kind of blackmail: that she knew some sort of secret. Abby herself had never told me any such thing. I was guessing that the secret was Millicent Whetstone.

"I really can't say. It's confidential."

"It's not confidential. It's Sebastian. If anybody says anything to Sebastian, you can forget the confidential part. He's incapable of keeping his mouth shut. He really is. I'm just about fed up with him."

Did I dare ask her what I wanted to know? Could I say: was your mother somehow involved with Morris Gross? I summoned up all my courage and asked the question, as gently, and as subtly as I could. But not gentle and subtle enough.

"Are you out of your mind?" she said. "They hated each other." Then it dawned on her. "Are you implying. . . . I can't believe this. . . . You think my mother had something to do with Morris Gross? I mean, his death? Is this Sebastian's idea?"

I had only enough time to say, "no, not Sebastian," before she slammed down the phone.

I had gotten nowhere. Probably calling her was a bad idea. I had certainly bungled it. And I had probably gotten Sebastian in trouble, although surely he could handle it Maybe I had just put an end to Sebastian's romance with Abby Whetstone. I had the feeling she would be furious with him.

Still, I wasn't particularly worried about Sebastian. I imagine he could replace Abby quickly, and he probably would.

Abby had been so positive about her mother. Was my hunch completely wrong? And if it was, what next?

22

It was time to take stock. Some of the mystery had been cleared up; some of it remained. After my conversation with Melrose Percival, for example, I knew all I needed to know about the death of Bertha Gross. Well, almost all.

Morris's strange will-making behavior: I think I understood that now. I had told him that a murderer, under California law (and most state laws) cannot inherit. Morris had only the vaguest conception of law; he also, for some reason that I really didn't understand at the time, was convinced he was responsible for his mother's death. Did he possibly think he was in danger of losing the money? Was that why he decided to cut everybody out of his will, and leave the money to charity? I thought this was likely.

But then, why did he change his mind? After his last conversation with Melrose Percival, I guess he finally came to terms with his guilt. He realized, too, that there was no danger he would lose the money. That's when he decided to make a new will. It also explains why he suddenly turned on Everett Mills. His sense of guilt had kept him from firing Everett Mills, or making a fuss about what Everett had done. Once the cloud of guilt had lifted, he turned on Mills and threatened to expose him.

The new will though—the do-it-yourself will, the holograph: he never consulted me about it. He put the family back into his will. But clearly, he was afraid of somebody—he wrote that other letter, the one that disappeared. He was afraid of someone, and his fears were justified. But who? What was going on in his muddled brain?

I had been thinking: maybe he was afraid of Millicent Whetstone. She knew something. And I thought she might have confided her secret to her daughter Abby. That was why Abby thought she could squeeze money out of Morris.

I felt excited. I had the feeling you get when you're sure you're right about something. But feelings can be awfully, awfully wrong.

I had lunch by myself the next day; I buried myself in a booth at my favorite Italian restaurant and tried to encourage my brain with ravioli smothered in clam sauce. As I was walking back to my office, I bumped into Sebastian. "Hi, Frank," he said. "I was looking for you."

"Well, you found me."

"Boy, you really pissed Abby off. She was ranting and raving last night. I thought she looked really terrific, all red and angry, you know, her whole body was moving and shaking, like wow. Sexy as all get out. She was smoking hot, I mean, I never saw her like that. I said, hey baby, calm down, but she actually hit me, and the next thing I knew, she was out the door."

"Sebastian: I'm sorry," I said.

"Don't be sorry. There's a lot of fish in the sea. Anyway: I got the impression, in between outbursts, that you thought it was her mother, you know, the one who got rid of Morris. Shot him dead. Cool! I love the idea. Millicent, she's quite a woman, I always thought so. Anyway, he deserved it, the old bastard. I mean, if she killed him, she must have had a reason, you know what I'm saying? I mean, it wasn't first-degree murder or that sort of thing. Maybe he tried to kill her, you know, and she shot him in self-defense. I'm crazy about Millicent. Maybe more than Abby. I know, she's old and all that. But Frank, do you have proof? About Millicent? Why do you think she's the one?"

"Sebastian," I said. "I don't have proof of anything. It's just an idea. A hunch. In a way, I'm sorry I brought it up. Really. To be honest, I did think maybe Millicent Whetstone is the one who did Morris in. You know, I think maybe she had something going with Morris, and, well, maybe it was a lover's quarrel."

"Her and that creep? Out of the question, Frank. I mean, the woman has taste. And Uncle Morris, I mean, I suppose he had a penis, after all, everybody does, not that I ever saw his, or wanted to—but I can't see him with Millicent. No, that woman has class. She wouldn't stoop that low. But really: Millicent? Seriously? And Bertha, too? I meant to ask you, do you think she killed Grandma?"

"Your grandma? No, I don't think so."

"Anyway, she wasn't even around, I know that. She was on a trip somewhere, Abby told me, I mean I checked the dates, because I remember Abby mentioning, her mother went on one of those cruises, Greek islands or some place in Europe. Or was it some other kind of cruise? She even met some guy on the boat, but nothing came of it, anyway, that's not the point. Of course, maybe she set up something before she left, you know, with the toothpaste. Something to get rid of Bertha. Of course, I don't know the motive. Not yet, anyway."

"Sebastian: forget the toothpaste," I said. "Nobody killed your grandmother."

"Do you want me to talk to Millicent?" he asked. "Find out, did she really kill Uncle Morris?"

"Sebastian, I beg of you: please don't."

I was hoping that he would be sensible, for once, and not confront Millicent. Also, I knew pretty much for a fact that nobody had actually killed Bertha Gross, not literally anyway, with or without toothpaste. So the fact that Millicent was away cruising the Mediterranean or wherever she had gone—that was totally irrelevant.

People believe in their hunches, and that includes me. But when a hunch turns out to be wrong, you have to be willing to give it up. If it wasn't Millicent, well, I had to rethink things. The night Bertha died, there was that five minute gap, the one Melrose Percival told me about. If Morris hadn't stepped across the hall to see Millicent Whetstone, what had he done? Most likely he was making a phone call. But to whom?

"If it wasn't Millicent," Sebastian said. "Maybe it was Aunt Anna. Frank, is that a better idea? I mean, she was the one who sent Johnny on that hike, you know, so he could throw away the gun and that other stuff."

"But that gun had nothing to do with Morris, Sebastian, remember that. And you said she was out, because she was family."

"OK, OK. But I could change my mind, couldn't I? See, here's the point: she didn't want *any* guns around. Look, Frank, this is what happened: she got really mad at Morris, I mean, who could blame her? Stupid fool that he was. He went around telling everybody, you're not getting my money, it's going to some idiotic charity, in memory of Bertha Gross, or whatever, as if anybody needed to remember the old crone. So something snapped, and she got rid of him. She had a key, so she let herself in, and they had a big fight, and she was furious, and, something snapped, she just lost it. Then she ditched the gun; that was the easy part. But she had another gun, and that would seem suspicious, right, Frank? So she told Johnny to get rid of that. And she had a hissy fit in the house and smashed stuff—that was suspicious, too. That's what happened. Should I talk to her?"

"I'm begging you, Sebastian, don't do it."

But he did.

23

Felicity called me the next day. She was tremendously agitated. "I swear," she said, "Sebastian, my dear brother, I could wring his neck. Frank, you've got to do something. He had some sort of conversation with Aunt Anna, and she's been in a state ever since. Can you come to her house, tonight, tomorrow, whenever? She has to talk to you."

That was easier said than done. Celia had invited her cousin over for dinner, and I knew it would be hard for me to skip out. This was a young cousin—actually, a cousin's daughter—named Chloe, who used to work for our dentist, but now was holding down some other sort of job. Fortunately, at the last minute, fate stepped in: Chloe cancelled, claiming she had a terrific headache. I have my suspicions that the headache was just an excuse, she had some other reason, possibly a young male reason . . . but I kept my thoughts to myself. I told Celia I was glad Chloe cancelled; I had an important business appointment.

Not that I was eager to confront Anna, under the circumstances. I arrived at her condo, in a pretty nervous state. I rang the bell, and she let me in. She looked totally distraught. She offered me coffee, which I turned down. We sat in the rather dim living room. "You can't imagine how painful all this has been," she said, half sobbing. "Morris dying, and . . . the *way* he died, it's so awful, police, questions, the whole thing is so sordid. We've always been respectable people. Mother was very strict, very strict. She was from the old school. She raised us that way."

"You wanted to speak to me," I said. Anna had a tendency to go off on tangents; and I certainly wasn't about to encourage her.

"I did. I know you've been talking about me. To Felicity, and Sebastian. But you just don't understand things. My heart is broken. I can't sleep at night. My blood pressure.... And nobody cares, nobody. I'm so lonely. And these suspicions. Sometimes I feel I'd be better off dead."

What could I say?

"My brother Morris ... we were close," she said, wiping away a tear. "Charlie, my other brother, rest in peace, he's dead and gone. And my dear sister, Martha, my only sister: she moved away. I was heartsick, you can imagine. So then there was only the two of us. Morris meant so much to me. Oh, Mother too of course. Anyway, before Mother died, I don't know exactly when, I'm not good at dates; anyway, Morris called me, and said he wanted me to come over. He said, I have something to tell Mother, she's not going to like it, and I want you to be there. So of course I went. I'll never forget that evening. It was so painful. Mother was sitting in the big easy chair, the one she always sat in. She said, what's Anna doing here? I said, just visiting, Mother. She said, I don't believe that, there's always a reason. Nobody comes to see me without a reason. Then Morris said, I asked her to come. I wanted her to hear what I have to say, Mother. And she said, what are you talking about? He said, Mother, I'm going to get married."

"Married?"

"That's what he said. I'm going to get married. Well, Mother, she had a fit. She said, you're not going to do anything of the sort. You're an old fool, Morris. I never heard such a thing. After all these years, you want to leave me and go off with some creature, after all I've done for you—given you a home, you never had to work, Morris, I'm your mother, and I absolutely forbid it."

"What did he say?"

"He said, Mother, people need to get married, Anna was married, Charlie, Martha.... She said, yes, and they all made a holy mess of it. But I simply won't have it, Morris. Not you.

Some gold-digger got hold of you, I know it. Charlie's dead, Martha moved God-knows where, and Anna here, she never comes by unless she wants something—Frank, that hurt me, when she said that, my own dear mother, but she could be very unfair. But she was terribly upset. Anyway, she said, you're all I have, Morris. I don't want to hear another word. And let me tell you, if you go through with this, you're not bringing that woman, whoever she is, in here—and you won't get a penny of my money. Not a penny. I'll throw you out on the street."

"And what did he say?"

"He said, all right Mother. What else could he say? And she said, I mean it, Morris. Not another word. I just won't have it. It was so awful, really. I never saw Morris look so unhappy. He was crushed. I went home. But I called him the next day, and said how sorry I was about all of this. I asked him, who she was, the woman he wanted to marry, and he said, you don't know her, never mind. It's over."

"And was it?"

"I don't know. I think it wasn't. I don't know how he was managing it, anyway; Mother watched him like a hawk. But I think—no, I know—that things really deteriorated from then on, it just wasn't the same, and then Mother died, and he told me later on, he felt guilty about Mother, felt he had killed her . . . he blamed himself for her death. I told him that was nonsense. He said, she left him all her money, she would have cut him out, that's why he couldn't get married. Now he had the money, but it was blood money, and he was going to leave it to charity. I was furious with him about that; I said, it's not fair, Morris. It wasn't fair on Mother's part, and it isn't fair on yours. But he wouldn't listen."

"When was this?" I asked. "When did you hear about this plan, I mean, that he was going to give all his money to charity."

"It was after he had that terrible heart attack. Oh, that was dreadful. My poor brother. It came out of the blue. I was so shocked when I heard the news, about his condition. I was afraid we were going to lose him. The poor man nearly died."

"Yes, I know that," I said.

"I visited him in the hospital every day, I didn't miss a day. At first, he was in this intensive care place, with all those tubes and things, and then he was in a room, with another man, awful person, another heart patient, that man was so sick, and he kept on wheezing and coughing. Anyway, I never missed a day, I brought Morris things he needed, and when he went home, he was still weak, I used to bring him food, soup, every day—Morris liked soup, especially lentil soup, I made sure he had his soup. He had a woman who came in to help out, terrible woman, she was from Samoa or somewhere, she must have weighed 400 pounds. I said, Morris, you don't need her when you have me, I'm your sister, and he said, what, Anna, are you going to take me to the bathroom, I'm paying this woman, she does what I want. One day, he said to me, Anna, I have to tell you something. I've had a kind of vision. I said, Morris, what do you mean, what kind of vision? He said, don't ask me about it, just listen. I have to make things up to my mother, it's not really my money, you wouldn't understand.

"I don't know what you're talking about, I said to Morris. He said, the money is going to charity. Don't ask questions. Well, I was disappointed, and hurt, but we never expected him to die, you know that. He kept saying, it has to do with Mother, and I had no idea why he was saying that. He just was. I still don't understand. And I thought: maybe that woman, maybe she has something to do with it. I wanted to talk to him about it, but he refused to say anything at all."

"They hadn't broken up?" I asked.

"Not then. But right before he died, he told me: things have changed. I'm not feeling guilty any more. I'm going to change my will, but it's a secret. I said, well, Morris, it's your money. He said, I know you and the rest of the family, I know you want that money, well, you'll get it, but you have to wait until I'm dead, and I said, oh Morris don't talk like that, you know we love you, and he just sneered, poor man, he found it so hard to express emotions. I tell you, it breaks my heart to think about it, because he *was* dead, and it was so soon. Right after he broke up with that woman."

"Did he?" I asked. "Did he break up with her?"

"He said he would. I don't know exactly why it happened. He said he had a conversation with Mel Percival, and he had changed his mind about all sorts of things. He was going to leave the money to his family. I told you that. And he was going to make a clean break with that woman. I'm going to tell her, it's all over, he said. I said, good, Morris, that's a good thing to do. And he said, I'm going to leave instructions in an envelope, in case she claims something, nowadays women can take your money if you're intimate with them, I read that in a magazine. I told him, I didn't think that was true, but he said, yes, it was in this article, they called it palimony or something, and I'm not taking any chances."

"And do you know if he carried through?"

"I think he did. Do you know, she was so brazen, she used to stay over there, in the condo. I mean, of course, after Mother died. But he was always careful, not to let any of us see her. She killed him. I'm sure of it. He told her he was finished, she was never getting his money, he would see to that, and she must have gone crazy, angry, and killed him. That's what happened. I just know that's true. She must have taken that envelope. And she took everything that would have given her away. Including her toothpaste."

"The toothpaste!"

"I should never have mentioned the toothpaste. I noticed the toothpaste when I was there. But there was other stuff, too. Some awful pills. Niagara, or whatever they call it. Men use it for sex, when they get old. I see it advertised on television. That was gone, too. And her toothbrush. I was foolish enough to say something to Felicity, and then when she repeated it, I made up a bunch of stuff, I didn't want people to know, because of the scandal, and also . . . because I was frightened. I didn't want her to know I knew about her. I didn't want her to kill me too. She took the envelope, I'm positive. But she'll never get any money. She knew that. That's why she did it."

"And the soapstone dish?"

"I smashed it. I was so angry. I didn't want her to have anything. I knew about the list . . . I saw it in Morris's house. I smashed that thing to pieces. But I didn't want her to know that. I've been scared to death. . . . I didn't dare say a word to the police. I had no proof, nothing. Just a guess. I'm still scared. What can I do?"

She hadn't mentioned a name; but I knew who she was referring to. And Abby had also known—that must have been the secret she held over Morris Gross's head. Not that he listened to her. Still, it must have strengthened his resolve, to get rid of the woman. Get her out of his life.

Yes, I knew who it was. And I also knew what to do. "Leave it to me, Anna" I said. "I'll take care of it."

"God bless you," she said.

24

I knew everything now, and it all made perfect sense. Morris had been carrying on with a woman. He even wanted to marry her. Bertha was furious when he told her. They had a terrific quarrel. She threatened to change her will, cut him out completely. Morris made promises, but then he broke those promises. Then came that awful evening. Bertha was going to change her will. She had summoned her lawyer and her accountant. She was probably threatening Morris. There might have been a terrible scene. Maybe she really did feel ill. And then, in the night, came the heart attack. Poor Morris didn't know what to do—or whether he could do anything. He called the woman; she no doubt told him to let his mother die. And she did die. Morris did not kill her, of course, but the incident preyed on his mind.

After she died, the affair continued. But it was rocky. The guilt was one thing. And, my guess is, that she kept pressuring him, about money, about an inheritance. He must have decided, it had to end. He broke it off abruptly; and then, in a rage, she killed him. That's what must have happened.

Here's what I did: first, I called Felicity, and told her what Anna told me. I told her what I thought had happened. And I asked her to pass it on to the police. They would listen to her story. She would tell them, that Morris had been involved with a woman, and that the two of them had had a bitter quarrel. That would be enough to make the woman a suspect.

And once you became a suspect, then sometimes everything falls into place. The police start investigating—once they have a name, and a motive, they look for evidence. And very often they find it.

This is exactly what happened. In short order, the police arrested Prudence Goldfinch, and charged her with the murder of Morris Gross. She had no alibi, she had a motive, she had a gun, and they found fingerprints in the apartment. She was the woman Morris Gross had called, when his mother was lying ill. Millicent Whetstone had seen her coming and going, in and out of the condo, after Bertha died. She told Abby, and Abby used that information. Or tried to. She got nothing for her pains.

No doubt all Prudence wanted was his money. Bertha was right all along.

A bachelor, or a widower, in his 60's, with money: men like this attract women like honey attracts bees. They are, after all, a rare commodity. The world is full of widows and divorcees. Bachelors and widowers with money—they're a rare commodity. Forget about high school quarterbacks: they're pikers with women compared to a well-off bachelor of 60.

In any event, Prudence seized her opportunity. She sank her claws into Morris. And when he turned on her, her anger knew no bounds.

There were still some loose ends, as far as I was concerned, but nothing major. My guess is that Morris lied to me—about going out of town—because Prudence was putting enormous pressure on him, pressure to get married, or to leave her his property, or something. And Morris resisted. He felt she was boxing him in. Maybe he liked having a girlfriend and using Viagra. But he was a selfish, cautious, narrow man; he felt he had gotten in too deep, and he reached the fateful decision, that Prudence would have to go. No wedding ring. No money. Nothing. Morris was through with her. Take your toothpaste and your toothbrush; and anything else, and get out.

But when he told her this, he never realized that he was signing his death warrant. Did she plan to kill him? Or was it a heat of passion sort of thing? I never found out.

After the police began to investigate, they built a strong case against her. Strong, but not airtight. But strong enough for them to arrest her and charge her with first degree murder.

She hired a good lawyer—one of the best. In the end, a deal was worked out. She pleaded guilty, but to manslaughter, not murder.

The estate of Morris Gross proceeded very smoothly. Sheppard, the accountant, was an enormous help, and there were no significant problems. I filed tax returns, took care of all the details, and, in due course, closed the estate. The heirs got their money. They were thrilled. I got my generous fee. The trip to Italy never materialized, but the Sub Zero refrigerator did: it sits proudly in our kitchen in gleaming stainless steel, giving birth to ice cubes at regular intervals. And the remodeling jobs—they're currently out for bids.

Anna wept when she got her check, and talked endlessly about her dear brother, and how much she missed him—how she would give up every penny just to have him back for one day. Nobody really believed her. And nobody was surprised when she moved into a nicer neighborhood and began buying expensive clothes.

Of course, Mrs. Leopold, at the building on Alma Street, was a most unhappy woman. Not only had there been a murder on the property, but the murderer was one of the residents. What Nobel prize-winner would want to live in a killer's apartment? The apartment of the murdered man—that was bad enough. We managed to sell it, though perhaps at a price a bit lower than it might have gone for otherwise. As for Prudence's apartment, I have no doubt that a buyer will appear in due course. Though perhaps not one with a Nobel Prize.

Once the assets had been distributed, my job was over. "Sebastian," I said, when I handed him a check and some papers to sign, "promise me you won't fritter this away. It's a lot of money. Try to be sensible."

He promised, but I have no faith in his promises. "I could produce a movie," he said. "Well, not a big movie, but one of those indies, like they have at Sundance. I always wanted to go there. Robert Redford goes there, I think. Those movies, they don't cost that much. I have a friend who's trying to write movie scripts. He's got one about zombies. I said, Justin, zombies are out; they've come and gone, just like vampires.

Nobody's doing vampires. Anyway, he's got talent and he has connections: he has a cousin who knows people in Hollywood. Maybe I can finance something there. I'd love to meet some movie stars. By the way, I'm dating Justin's sister. She's really hot. Oh, and yes, Frank, I'm still thinking about detective work. I wasn't so far off, was I, about the toothpaste? Of course, I had no way of knowing about that Prudence woman. It was her toothpaste, right? So I was on the right track, Frank, wasn't I?"

Who knows what track Sebastian is on. I wish him luck in life. He might need it.

They're all rich now: Anna, Sebastian, Felicity, Julia, and Martha. If they need a lawyer, for estate planning or any other purpose, I'm available. I think they were happy with my work. They still think of me as a great detective, but they also, I hope, think of me as a competent lawyer. If they need legal services, I'm definitely available. I'd be happy to have them as clients. But please, no murders.

Also by Lawrence Friedman, more QP Mysteries, in the series *The Frank May Chronicles:*

Death of a Wannabe

An Unnatural Death

The Book Club Murder

Death of a One-Sided Man

Who Killed Maggie Swift?

About the author

Lawrence Friedman is a professor of law at Stanford University. He teaches courses in American legal history and law and society. He is the author of *A History of American Law*, *Crime and Punishment in American History*, *The Human Rights Culture*, and *Total Justice*, among other works. He recently published *Dead Hands: A Social History of Wills, Trusts, and Inheritances*, a subject which is the backbone of Frank May's (fictional) practice.

Visit us at *www.qpbooks.com.*